By Mike Heffernan

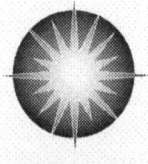

[silverthought]
PHILADELPHIA | NEW YORK

Praise for

"Toys with the dichotomy of our competing thrusts for liberty and subjugation and exposes the falseness of those who profess to save and of those who say they want to live... Explosive!"
— John Everson, from his introduction

"*Exposed!* shines a harsh light on the myriad horrors of modern society and reports back from the fearful frontlines with wicked wit and paranoid power. *Exposed!* is the last headline we get to read before reality comes tumbling down."
— Jeremy Robert Johnson, author of *Extinction Journals* and *Angel Dust Apocalypse*

"Delivers a heady mélange of Swiftian satire ended with the outré oddness of Caro and Jeunet's cinematic outings. *Exposed!* imagines a world where celebrities are hunted down for crimes of narcissism, the elderly and insane are processed like psychedelic chattel, and labor conflicts are worse than ever. Must-read stuff for the post-apocalyptic set."
— B.H. Fingerman, author of *Recess Pieces* and *Bottomfeeder*

"Among the 'writers to watch' in the realm of strange storytelling. Interrogates the hazy borderland between the human and the inhumane... A crafty form of social commentary."
— Michael A. Arnzen, author of *Play Dead* and *Grave Markings*

Printed in the United States of America.

Published by Silverthought Press.
www.silverthought.com

ISBN-10: 0-9774110-9-5
ISBN-13: 978-0-9774110-9-2

To those who've possessed my sprit and challenged my mind:
Barker, King, Ketchum, Banks, Orwell, Romero.

"We shall meet in a place where there is no darkness."
— George Orwell, *1984*

"The only good bourgeois is a dead bourgeois."
— Pol Pot

"It takes a certain mind to find beauty in a hamburger bun."
— Ray Kroc, founder of McDonald's

You know what scares the bejesus out of me? Control. Maybe I live in a paranoid plastic bubble, but goddamn, nothing scares me more than control—the personal, the political, the emotional. What about control? Well, there's the control the government and corporations like to hold over us, with their greasy fingers probing all aspects of society like a sneaky prostate exam, the control money and personal finances dictate the paths our lives take, the control the people around us try to hold as tight as a vice. I could go on. The loss of control, just as devastating as a disenfranchised and anonymous Joe Blow who mows down a restaurant full of families in the name of some personal revolution, frightens me even more.

To put it simply, I want to be working the switch of my own personal destiny and pulling the plug when it's time to kick it. At least that's how I like to think it'll all go down.

Control. That's what this collection is about, in more ways than one. And no one wrote about the topic more articulately than George Orwell did. Maybe, just maybe, if it weren't for *1984*, I'd still be writing about dark closets and things that go bump in the night.

Mike Heffernan

Table of Contents

Horror at the Oppressive Heart of Liberation

an introduction by John Everson

Right now there are bombs going off all around me. It's the 4th of July, the celebration of a nation's independence if you're here in the States, which is ironic, since I'm here to tell you about a Canadian writer. As a Canuck, it wouldn't seem that Mike Heffernan would have an investment in "Independence Day"... and yet... the title story of this collection starts off on June 22, which in Heffernan's world is a national holiday that sounds suspiciously like the one Americans are celebrating outside my house right now—Liberation Day.

But liberation, as any history-conscious American knows, comes with a cost. And Mike knows all about cost. *Exposed!* offers ten examples of the terrible cost of liberation: the cost of societal and personal freedom, the cost of love, the cost of delusion. In delving into the hidden core of those costs, he offers us an exploration, and in some cases, a promise, of liberation. But Mike's no fool. He knows that liberation—freedom—is not the natural order of humanity. In each of these tales, the dark nature of humanity is given its due. *Exposed!* Revealed for the evil duplicitous shadow dweller that it is. Quite often, the real result of "liberation" is oppression.

In the collection's leadoff title story, "Exposed," Heffernan paints a world not unlike that of Stephen King's "Running Man." But in this dark universe, the "runners" are former celebrities now scrambling to hide from their former notoriety. And the good folk—the old and infirm—are their ironically potent enemy as they watch a game show that combines the violence of "Running Man" with "America's Most Wanted."

But the violence of America's Most (un)Just can be subtle. And Mike doesn't let us take the easy road in *Exposed!* He doesn't flinch from the indefatigable hunger of the spurned homeless or the hopelessness of surviving the cataclysmic flood when what awaits on the side of life is a Cthulhu-esque leviathan hungry for the survivors. He will make you seethe with the cold fury of helplessness along with those who have literally given up their limbs for the cause only to find their selflessness scorned.

The latter exploration comes in "Cold Deck," one of the volume's most effective explorations of the (in)human condition. In it, Heffernan imagines a society where the men have literally replaced their limbs with saws and other logging implements to become the most effective tools for their jobs. And in typical human fashion, the faceless corporation that benefited from their dedication leaves them behind. And in typical human fashion, the women, not the men, take the decisive retributive action.

While the denizens of "Cold Deck" may be hapless victims of the uber-machine, the lead character of "Stains of Life" is a willful acceptor of enslavement. Here, Heffernan paints another dystopia—a land where the government imprisons and exploits drug users. Except that *before they were imprisoned, they weren't hooked on the stuff.* Again, freedom, liberation, is a central theme. And the personal decision on whether to choose freedom—at the potential price of death—is played out in a haunting denouement.

Another key theme for Mike is that while everything may look cozy... the acceptance of a veneer of happiness is dangerous. While everyone in "Stains of Life" is getting their fix, one character says, "Don't let appearances fool you. It isn't as innocent as it looks... This is a terrible place."

Indeed.

None of Mike's stories are as innocent as they may appear at first glance. They are terrible places, made so because they live close to where we live now; they are places that are only two steps to the right of today. It's not so hard to see the drug-concentration camps come true. Or the corporate genocide, of sorts, of a whole adapted blockade of workers. Or the persecution of an entire societal segment via a TV show.

Mike knows that we persecute difference and manufacture difference as an excuse to persecute. Liberation is not our natural state; oppression is.

He also knows that appearances lie. In Heffernan's fiction, it's deadly to dig through the smooth, masking walls to discover the truth of what's really going on behind them.

And truth is really at the heart of seeking, of living, isn't it? Mike has a strong sense of dark humor, and in "Open 24/7" he postulates an Art Bell scenario that would appeal to anyone who has spent several days with insomnia. Perhaps there *are* things out there waiting to help us. But help us accomplish... what, exactly? Is it really the truth that those things unveil? Or is it something worse? More primal?

The lies of the media's portrayal of human physical perfection underscore "Starved to Death," which finds a fat woman being helped, somewhat forcefully, to achieve her weight goals. But is it really what she wants? And when she gets there, what will she desire next?

Outside of my office right now, there are a thousand snaps, crackles and pops from hundreds of illegal fireworks (you are not supposed to own them here in Illinois). There are more than a few window-rattling bangs. In its illegal celebration of freedom shines the evidence of a society in love with itself for rebelling. For standing apart. For seeking liberation. Never mind that it is also a society that has an inexplicable tendency to squash the independence it celebrates in any who don't follow the majority.

In the following pages, you'll find the evidence of a writer who toys with the dichotomy of our competing thirsts for liberty and subjugation. Mike Heffernan exposes the falseness of those who profess to save and of those who say they want to live... but choose dying. *Exposed!* offers a series of stories that have the horror of reality at their core. They are all of them explosive. Small firecrackers that show you the now and the maybe and then... bang.

Savor the sparks. For in the fright of the fire burns the seed of change.

John Everson
July 4, 2006
Darien, IL

Exposed!

Jake—was Jerry; now Jake—had the day off. Everyone had the day off. Even the banks were closed. Children were out in the parks playing, there was a parade planned, a telethon took pledges for the underprivileged.

It was June 22, a national holiday. *Liberation Day*.

He recalled that first June 22 regularly, like his parents recalled Pearl Harbor or the day JFK was shot. As he sat in his hospital room, watching television with a growing sense of dread, men in dark suits had stormed *The Aubrey Winter Show* brandishing automatic rifles. Tim Crewe, the guest, hair slick, teeth gleaming white under the soft lighting, there to promote some new action blockbuster, to talk about his budding love life, sat staring, an unmistakable dark patch quickly spreading out from the crotch of his jeans and growing to the size of a dinner plate, as one of the assailants put a rifle to the back of Aubrey's head, pulled the trigger. There was a loud crack, one simultaneous gasp from the audience, and the camera shook and went out of focus, facing down like a dead animal. When it finally centered on the stage again, it showed Tim, covered in blood and brain tissue and bits of teeth, still staring, still unmoving, no longer the suave and handsome movie star. Aubrey, a fist-sized hole punched through her face where her nose had

17

once been, slumped to the side. Tim's co-stars were then brought out on stage, handcuffed, shackled at the ankles, looking like they'd been beaten to an inch of their lives. Tim was then thrown to the ground, restrained, kicked in the ribs for good measure, brought to stand in line with them.

One of the assailants, a red sash running across his chest, obviously in charge, reached into his jacket and produced a plain sheet of paper, started reading. "According to Section 6b of the *Constitution of the New Order*, you have been charged and found guilty of 'Crimes against the Cultural Integrity of the Nation.'"

Quiet, defeated, confused, the actors were marched off stage, Tim in the lead.

For a moment, the screen went blank, grey and dull, like winter clouds carrying sleet in from the ocean.

Pictures then began to flash: wanted signs, portraits, the kind agents use to hook their clients roles. Brief physical descriptions and known aliases rolled across the bottom. All the major Hollywood stars were there, all guilty, all wanted. The rewards for their capture were steep.

Jake had flicked through the channels, hoping to find a tidbit of info, some small smidgen of news. Nothing. All the stations were the same, putting out the same signal.

It was at that moment that Muriel ran in, crying, hysterical, hands ripping at her hair. Her face was covered in clean white bandage, adhesive tape spreading out across her cheeks. Nose job, like Jake. She'd asked him to leave— no, *begged* him. She was the face of weather on *Channel-9 Rochester*; he was the sports. Small town celebrities, both of them, with aspirations of something more, something bigger. "They've killed Aubrey! *Aubrey*, for God's sake. Why, Jake, why? How could they kill that good woman?"

"I don't know. I don't know," he said, getting out of bed.

Up and down the hallway, patients and staff were glued to television sets, some crying, some holding hands in front of their mouths, eyes wide.

A few, winter coats hauled over hospital gowns, raced past, dragging their suitcases, pajamas and socks hanging out and flapping behind them. Jake grabbed one woman by the wrist. She had her head wrapped lengthways from a recent chin lift. "Have you seen the TV? Do you know what's going on?"

"It's a takeover. Had my husband on the line. They were at the door; they're after me, you know. They're after *all* of us. I'm getting away while I still can. Canada, maybe. You'd best do the same."

That was four years ago.

Eight apartments ago.

Six Hack-shacks, two infections, seven skin grafts ago.

Since then, his picture had appeared on television only once: the old Jerry, the handsome Jerry, the *criminal* Jerry. He'd barely even recognized himself.

Each evening, the state ran its most popular show, *EXPOSED!* Former celebrities, the small time and the big time, completed humiliating, murderous, savage tasks: Russian roulette, sword fights, fire walking. A national phenomenon, ratings soared.

So much changed.

Popular entertainment was outlawed, abolished, erased.

Churches, mosques, synagogues: burned.

Video stores, indoor malls: ransacked, the employees sent to the colonies.

Politicians, business leaders, CEOs: tortured.

But the old and infirm, the poor, were powerful symbols and afforded opportunity, comfort.

Under forty, unimportant, Jake occupied a one-bedroom state-issued flat on the lower east side, small, cramped, roach infested, the dank hallways smelling of boiled cabbage and sour breath. On Monday, Wednesday and Saturday evenings, he sat with Mrs. Jorgensen. Law required all citizens over the age of twenty-one to serve as part-time companions to the elderly. With her for six months, those afternoons were not unpleasant for Jake— her refrigerator consistently full, her apartment warm and comfortable.

Kind, talkative, she enjoyed watching *EXPOSED!*

Today: Wednesday. Despite the human traffic on the streets, thousands clogging the sidewalks, anticipating the floats, the government officials waving from convertibles, Mrs. Jorgenson waited, as always, television tuned in to *EXPOSED!*

She had tea steeping. "Have you heard? They've finally caught Martin Downton Jr."

Surprised: "Really?" He sat in his usual spot, the recliner.

Downton was there, onscreen, ushered out from behind the red curtain, looking like Ted Kaczynski: hair long and tangled, dirt and leaves collected in his beard, clothes tattered and worn, skin grey and mottled. Confusion and fear were pasted all over him. Hulking guards flanked him on either side, making him look small, pathetic, wounded.

"Where was he found?"

Mrs. Jorgenson poured cream. "In the sewers, like the *rat* he is."

The announcer listed off his crimes, everything from promoting immoral behavior to prostitution. The usual. Nothing new there.

"You must remember him. He was a real piece of work, he was, that Downton fellow."

Jake thought the man had been savvy, a real crooner, ahead of his time. Admitting it would be criminal. "Yes, he was a piece of work, alright. At least he's caught." VHS tapes floated around on the black market. Dangerous stuff. Prized pieces. Episodes of *The Martin Downton Jr. Show* weren't cheap. He had heard them go for as much as $150 a pop.

The camera zoomed out and showed a swimming pool. The announcer, loud and billowing, said it was filled with bilge water. The challenge: Downton was to dive in, find a key at the bottom and unlock his shackles.

The guards poked him with an electric cattle prod and moved him to the edge. His toes dangled over.

They gave him a final zap, and he fell in, belly-flopping, quickly disappearing beneath.

Bubbles surfaced.

Seconds passed.

Mrs. Jorgenson smiled, hands tucked beneath her legs, rocking in anticipation. "Oh, this is exciting."

Downton finally emerged, mouth gaping, trying to grab a breath, screaming. Hands flailing and thrashing, "Jesus, sweet Jesus! *My eyes!* I can't see! They're burning! Jesus, *Jesus!*"

The camera zoomed in and focused on his face and showed hot coals where his eyes once had been, burned out and swollen. But the key was there, grasped tightly in his right hand.

The guards used a fishnet to haul him out.

The screen went blank. Grey again. *73-EXPOSED,* green neon block letters, flashed across the bottom. *CALL NOW AND RECEIVE AN ADDITIONAL REWARD!* Then more images and wanted signs.

The two watched intently, sipping tea and nibbling sugar biscuits that Mrs. Jorgenson had baked.

"Those pictures are useless," she commented. "They're all a decade old. We need something else. Voice recordings, maybe."

Jake nodded in agreement. "The tea is delicious. All we get is the stale stuff back at the flats."

"I'm glad you like it, dear. It's the least I can do."

Sipping, watching the screen, Jake saw it, his picture, over the edge of the cup: old, worn. He was young, at the

21

start of his career. Barely recognizable. Before television, just doing off, off Broadway. He still had the goatee, nose crooked—leaning to the left—hair gelled straight back, not cropped short and whipped to the side.

"God," Mrs. Jorgenson gasped. "Says he's suspected of a number of offences."

The tea went down in one hard lump, like thick dough. For a moment, it caught in his throat, and he was unable to breathe. *Calm down, she'll never know. That was a decade ago. You've been in worse binds than this, anyway. Play it cool. Don't sweat it.* He swallowed the tea; forced it down. *There. Make some comment. Keep talking. But don't force it.* "Men like that are worse than the biggies. They're *still* dangerous." *There. Nice one. Keep it up, but don't overdo it.* "They're able to hide in public. People forget about them."

The elderly were routinely given vacations abroad, moved to high-rise apartments as rewards for turning in their companions, their neighbors, their children. They were the worst, especially the widowed. Like snakes in tall grass: always on the hunt.

"I suppose you're right."

There. She didn't notice a thing.

"June Beresford, you know, the lady three doors down, the one with the bad hip, she turned in her companion last week. Thought he was one of them on the television. They took him away. Don't know what happened to him, but she got a new sofa set out of it. Guess he was guilty of something. I could use a new sofa set." She laughed, patted Jake on the leg. "But you're a good boy. You'd never have gotten mixed up in that sort of thing: money and fame."

Jake felt sweat drip down his back. His heart did double time; he was sure she could hear it, see his shirt push out. *You look nothing like that, buddy. Got that nose fixed. The hair cut short. Even lost fifty pounds. Nothing like that. Don't worry. Remember Johnston, huh? Next door, remember? Even when the cops called, came and inquired about him, they didn't spot you. If they didn't, she won't.*

The television went blank.

Jake gulped the last of his tea, got up from the recliner. "Well, time for me to head off. They've got me on a road crew tomorrow morning. Not so bad. I'll be out in the sun, at least."

"Friday evening, then? They're having a trash-rag burning after *EXPOSED!* They located a huge stash of them in a black market warehouse by the docks. Oh, it should be exciting. I don't get much excitement."

Jake laughed, kissed her cheek. "Of course, Mrs. Jorgenson. And thank you for the tea and cookies. They were wonderful, as always."

"And, please, take the subway tonight, dear. Seeing those men there on the television has got my nerves going." She sighed.

She saw him to the door.

"I will," Jake said, moving into the hallway. "Friday, then?"

"Friday."

The Daily Telegram opened on his cot. Snipping pictures out and pasting them in one of his scrapbooks, filled with old publicity photos, now mug shots, like on television, turned ugly.

Jake had his taped to the bathroom mirror, comparing himself now to the old, former Jake, inspecting his nose, behind his ears, across the hairline, along his neck, searching for signs of scarring. Found none, not so much as a faint red line. The hack shops had done some good work on him.

Muriel was there, too, on page four, book five. *His* Muriel. He kept a copy beneath the mattress and stared at it often, took it to bed, imagined she was there with him, beneath the sheets, holding him.

Red crosses ran through half of the pictures. It was his way of keeping track, recording who'd been caught, which of his former colleagues were still out on the streets, or featured on *EXPOSED!* Muriel's was untouched. He wondered if she'd gone underground or was a companion for someone like Mrs. Jorgenson. Probably. Maybe she'd made it across the border.

(Please, God, let it be.)

Doubtful. Few had made it. She probably had work done, too: nose straightened, chin partially reconstructed, brow lifted. He wondered if he'd even recognize her now, or she him.

Confessions, which were printed in the papers like epitaphs, frightened him, too. They were experts in torture, the agents of the government. Before *EXPOSED!*, weeks, months, maybe, they kept you in a rat hole of a cell, beaten, electrified, whatever it took to get your tongue moving the way they wanted: names, addresses, descriptions. *If they get Muriel, will she tell them I'm still out here? Where will I go then? Can't stay here, I know that. I'll have to get out of the city somehow.*

Social assistance, the road crew, squalor, visiting the woman, the ever-present fear, he was used to them now, used to most everything. It all changed you, too, made you into something else, something you only recognized sometimes, not wholly you. Things once alien, abhorred, Jake would do now in an instant, without thinking, instinctive. He'd killed. Killed the sound tech from *Channel-9 Rochester* in a greasy alley with a broken beer bottle. He had wanted money to keep quiet.

Jake lay on his cot. Lit a marijuana cigarette, coughed, felt his head get light as his lungs filled with rich smoke. Legalized, much cheaper than cigarettes, the government figured they kept people subdued, compliant, *content.* He thought of the sound tech and how he'd opened up his throat, watched blood jet out between his clutching fingers, his eyes blaring mad.

The sound tech had been young, a boy, really, seduced by rewards.

Images of him lying in a heap of garbage in the gutter haunted Jake. He could do it again, unflinchingly. He figured he was not alone. Murder rates had soared in the last few years, since *EXPOSED!*

The old woman had broken her ankle getting out of the bath, requiring surgery. During her two-week stay in hospital, Jake recorded each night's episode of *EXPOSED!*

He visited her three times a week, talked, drank the stale coffee from the machine in the lobby.

On his first visit, her mind cloudy with pain and morphine, she touched his hand, her skin soft like tissue paper, told him he reminded her of her younger brother. He had left for Vietnam but hadn't returned. Volunteered. Stupid. With all her money, she couldn't keep him home.

"Money?" Jake asked.

Glassy-eyed, voice sluggish like oatmeal: "Enough to wipe my ass with." Then she slipped under, her head turned to the side, towards the IV, as if hypnotized by the drip.

He quickly scanned the old photos clipped from *The Daily Telegraph*, a thick pile already scattered on the floor. Would he even recognize her, if she *were* there? The question loomed. Forty, fifty years may have passed. She would be young, vibrant. And who was to say that bribes hadn't been made, payoffs placed? It wasn't unheard of.

For hours, he flipped page after page, passed over hundreds of headlines, fingers black with old ink, brain buzzing mad from lack of sleep.

Dawn crept up the wall through the blind, slashing it into two dozen pieces.

Get up. Have a drink, man, and then sleep. The crew can do without you today.

Reaching for the bottle, newspapers fell to the floor. He took two long, hard pulls off the bottle, a third for good measure. The sour liquor burned his throat, warmed his gut.

Then he saw it, mocking him, staring up from the floor. It read like a 1940s noir cliché: *FAMILY FORTUNE GOES UP IN SMOKE: HEIRESS MISSING, PRESUMED DEAD.*

Jake turned the tracking with his thumb, watched the streaks and slashes of silver fade to dull grey. Contestants became visible. Voices audible, their bodies no longer moved in quick spasmodic jerks.

Hit rewind. Background black, *EXPOSED!* flashed across the length of the screen.

He sat back and nibbled on a biscuit.

Mrs. Jorgensen, excited: "Oh, I'm glad you managed to tape the shows for me. I really appreciate it, Jake. I'll be sure to tell them what a wonderful job you've done when your next review comes up. You've been such a dear."

Flashing a smile: "No problem. That's what I'm here for."

The night's contestants—two of them—had been professional athletes. They were brought out and made to stand at the starting line of an indoor track: one hundred meters, carpeted in broken glass.

No shoes.

The announcer's voice came on, told them they had to come in at under twenty seconds. The contestants dripped icy sweat. Hopping from foot to foot, eyes darting at one another nervously, they squatted down, squared their shoulders, and took one last look up the length of track, at each other, the glass glinting in the lights.

"I'll bet one of them makes a break for it." Mrs. Jorgensen laughed.

Four red digital zeros appeared at the bottom right-hand corner of the screen.

The pistol fired, and the contestants sprang.

The one on the inside never missed a step, arms and legs pumping, chest heaving in steady rhythms, glass crunching beneath his feet with each stride, digging into his soles, and splashing blood. The other had already tripped and was splayed out on the track, crying, clutching his feet as the clock ticked off seconds.

The red digits stopped at *18.56*.

Mrs. Jorgensen clapped. "Oh, God! Can you believe it? Can you *believe* he made it? And less than twenty seconds. The man almost deserves to be let free."

The other contestant, dragged back through the glass and to the start again, was told to run again.

To Jake, the outcome seemed obvious. "He's not running."

Mrs. Jorgensen, hands beneath her legs, neck craned forward in anticipation: "He'll run. He'll run. He might not make it all the way, but he'll run."

Another shot rang off. The camera zoomed in. The contestant looked weak, starved, something Jake hadn't noticed before, but his strides were strong this time, long, and he was making good time. The fifty-meter mark zipped past. Then, abruptly, he tripped again, fell, shrieked. Lifting his head, hands outstretched, face sliced up into a thousand-piece jigsaw puzzle, glass poked out of his skin, driven in deep from the fall.

A guard appeared behind him and raised a rifle to the back of his head, the other guard already there with a long trolley, body bag rolled out and unzipped. Usually these things were left off-camera, replaced by military recruitment ads.

Jake and Mrs. Jorgensen looked at one another and shrugged their shoulders. They continued watching, waiting for the crack of the rifle and muzzle-flash and for the contestant to slump forward as his brain exited his forehead in a spray of pink.

The television faded to black.

They sighed.

EXPOSED! flashed across the screen, then photos appeared physical descriptions.

"I think we'll see that first contestant again, that one who finished. You don't find entertainment like *that* very often. Did you see the look in his eyes? Savage. I can only imagine what he's guilty of."

"They didn't say, did they?"

"No, I don't think so."

Jake sipped the last drop of his tea. Enjoyed the sugary sludge at the bottom, and licked his lips. Sugar was rare; no sugar in the flats, not for any of the companions.

"Fast-forward, would you, dear?" Mrs. Jorgensen asked. "I don't care too much for the fugitive updates anymore. All the same old stuff."

Jake went to the television and hit fast-forward. Faces appeared in quick succession, like a slideshow.

Then he saw her: Muriel. *Muriel. His* Muriel.

Eyes fixed, the tape seemed to have paused itself, freeze-framed for eternity.

Looking fit, her skin tanned, hair now long and curly: a police photo, not the cropped family photo he had that was taken before her surgery, before June 22, the same photo he kept beneath the floorboards, the photo he kissed at night, smelled, outlined with his fingertips, prayed to.

Six thousand was being offered for her capture. It flashed at the bottom, green dollar signs on either side, like a late-night infomercial from years past.

(*Jesus! High; too high. They'll all be out after her.*)

She'd been caught trying to cross the border, then escaped, killing two guards in the process.

Mrs. Jorgensen: "Pause! *Pause!*"

He hit the button and felt his stomach loosen up inside, waited for it to fall out the other end.

Pointing at the screen with her gnarled arthritic finger, poking it forward in a jabbing motion: "I know her. I know her! By Christ, I know her. She was the nurse at the

28

hospital. Volunteer, I think. That's her, the one that brought me my breakfast. Laura was her name."

Laura. Was Muriel; now Laura.

She'd been in the city all this time. Near, only miles, blocks away from him. At the hospital, he might have passed right by her, brushed against her, smelled her, eyed her.

There was the click, click, click of the rotary phone being dialed.

Jake turned.

Mrs. Jorgensen had the phone to her ear, eyes wide, biting down on her lip and enjoying the taste. She was calling the toll-free hotline, waiting for the operator.

"What are you doing?" Jake asked, words coming out slow and hard, monosyllables.

Hand over the receiver: "You know what I could do with that money? I could get out of the city, move to the country. You could come with me, Jake. Think, away from all the people, the smoke, the crime. Wouldn't that be wonderful?"

"Put the phone down."

"What? Why? Why would I do that? Imagine this Laura woman on *EXPOSED!* They'd probably announce our names and everything. How exciting!"

Jake got up, walked to her, took the phone from her ear and put it back on its cradle. Looking down at her: "You're not calling anyone, Mrs. Jorgensen. I'm sorry."

"What... What are you talking about, Jake?"

Voice firm, confident, the voice he'd practiced in front of the bathroom mirror a dozen times, just in case things came to this: "Here's how it's going to be, and listen close. I know your name. I know you've got money stashed away. I know you're wanted, a fugitive. You're old, but I recognize you. You're going to cough up some cash, and lots of it, or I'm picking up the phone myself. And at your age, you wouldn't last long in custody, or in the colonies. We clear?"

Her head went low. Eyes welling up, nodding, she looked defeated. A whisper: "I understand."

"Good. Good."

"The money is in a safe under the bed, hidden beneath the floor. Key's in the top drawer of my dresser."

Jake yanked the phone out from the wall and went and got the safe. It was there, where she'd said. Heavy, he put it down on the floor, stared at it for a moment. "No tricks in store for me, right?"

"No. No tricks."

He slid the key into the lock, heart pounding hard like a machine, and opened the small metal door.

For a moment, he saw the dark muzzle of the gun looking up at him from inside, fixed in place, a trap. Its eye, black and emotionless, blinked, a flash of fire blinding his right eye, and he was sent back against the couch, clutching his face, flopping, heels drumming on the carpet.

Mrs. Jorgensen dialed the rotary. "Hello, I'd like to report *two* sightings."

"Don't..."

"Hello. I'd like to report two sightings. Yes, *two*. Where? Oh, the first is in my apartment. It's my companion. I saw his picture a few weeks back. No, I wasn't sure. I've shot him, so you'd best hurry. He looks to be in a bit of a ways. The other one? I saw her on the television, too. She works at a hospital in the city, and I recognized her. I know. That's right. I can't believe my luck, either. I'm on a pension, you know."

"Yes, folks," the announcer started, "you asked, and we heard you loud and clear!"

Fake applause, clapping, and sharp whistles roared. *EXPOSED!* flashed at the bottom of the screen. More clapping, hoots, hollers.

"Tonight's feature: *LOST LOVERS REUNITED!*"

A couple was escorted out from behind the long stage curtain by a dozen armed guards, thick leather collars tight around their necks—leashes—hands and feet shackled. Grey sacks had filled beneath their eyes, making them appear old and used up, spent. Clothes in tatters, stained in dark patches that looked black on the colorless TV. A dirty bandage—face wrapped tight—was visible each time the man shifted to his left and grimaced in pain.

Mrs. Jorgensen was ecstatic. Pointing at the screen of her new wall-mounted television: "That's him! That's him! That's Jake."

"You must be excited," Mrs. Beresford remarked. "I know I was. It's such an honor, isn't it?"

"I did my duty, that's all."

The camera followed the two contestants, panning the length of the stage as they scuffed along. A cage appeared, top closed. Solid steel bars reached to the ceiling. Restraints undone, led in through a door in the side then locked behind them, the couple were handed lethal looking weapons: machete, baseball bat with a dozen long and vicious nails driven through at the end.

The clock appeared at the bottom right-hand portion of the screen. Zeros flashed. Once, twice...

Mrs. Jorgensen leaned forward, excited.

The familiar buzzer shrilled.

The first and only round started, the clock counting down from ten minutes.

For a moment, quiet. Neither of the contestants moved. They stood staring at their weapons, each other.

The two old women could see Jake word something, an *I love you*, maybe.

Suddenly, the woman, his lover, smiled, held it for a second, raised the weapon over her head, ran forward, screaming, crazed, face a mask of hate and fear.

Jake put the machete on the floor, submitted. Eyes closed, he waited

"Oh, here it comes!" Mrs. Beresford exclaimed, biting her fingernails, already considerably gnawed down, and clutched the seat cushion.

The television switched cameras and went to a medium two-shot. The woman was there, already, and in one quick motion, she brought the bat down onto the crown of his head, stepped back and watched in horror as two thick jets of blood pumped up and arced into the air like a water fountain, his one good eye floating up. He touched his head, the bat, fingers running over the nails as if he were reading Braille, looked at his fingers dripping red, slumped slowly to his knees and fell face-first against the stage. His legs jerked once, twice, then he was still. Dead.

The screen went blank; the title appeared, flashed in green neon: *EXPOSED!*

"Now *that* was entertainment," Mrs. Jorgensen said, laughing, dabbing tears from her eyes.

Hard as Rock

He licked his split lips, ran his tongue over his toothless gums, and counted the fingers on both his hands.

One. Two. Three.
One. Two. Three. Four.

Counting them kept him steady, thinking, awake.

He could see them, his fingers, barely stubs, poking up through the holes of his soiled winter gloves, blackened like badly burned wieners, carbonized. They were mysterious creatures, alien. He could not feel them, yet they moved, as if someone across the street was controlling them through a remote. There had been a slight burning sensation in them that morning that had grown to a deep throbbing late in the afternoon, increasing as the temperature dropped well below freezing.

Low, faint, barely a memory, he wished for the pain to return, for his seven digits to say, *Don't worry, old buddy. We'll be around for a bit.*

He wanted to get up, walk, but was unable. His right leg was busted and cracked beneath his frozen and stiff pants. The bone poked at the skin just above his knee. The black ice was lethal, knew all the right places to hide, to lurk, and seemed to get more cunning with the passing of each year. It'd snuck up on him, the *bastard*, and caught him off guard. *Stupid!* Sending him pirouetting, somersaulting in the air, until he lay sprawled out on the downtown sidewalk, a swastika of pain, rolling and crying and withering. The late night bar crowd had come pouring out of the clubs, screaming, pushing, laughing, kicking, pouring beer over his face, parading past him as he clawed at the concrete.

To get to where he was, propped up inside this huge wooden box, had taken hours. Having to break through the boards was murder, putting them back into place torturous. All just so he could stay hidden, rest some.

The sleeping bag was soggy, wet; bits of it had frosted over. Wind whipped around inside, driving the cold into the centre of his head like a railroad spike. He watched a rusted-out Lysol bottle float by through the hole—the dirty lot a reservoir of silver slush. He wondered if it was empty. He'd do anything for a drop.

He thought of the truck, once his home, looking like a dead or dying animal, its guts, the motor, hauled out, the hood torn off. The slashed front seat, the broken radio that spewed red wires. Listening to the rain hit the roof like a thousand drumming fingers had given him comfort.

But it was a dream now, beyond time, a fleeting memory from early childhood that slipped between flashes of consciousness. The truck had been hauled off on the back of some ugly and massive machine-beast, leaving him out in the cold, to huddle in the doorways of banks and closed shops until they reopened, leaving him to crawl back to this wasteland lot, to the nothingness that was left of it.

He had never felt so utterly alone, deserted.

He wondered if the hard, burly men with the red plastic heads would return in the morning, to toss him somewhere else.

Blue tarpaulin, covering everything—machines, tools, massive wooden boxes like this—whipped and snapped with the wind, hypnotic. He blinked, and the Lysol bottle was gone, floated away. Sleep was creeping up, clutching at him with its big, lazy hands, promising some relief from the pain. His dog, Grey, had slept, was still sleeping; the winter, *this* winter, had been too much for him, the hunger too much for him, for him and Grey. The Country Chicken people used to give him scraps. But they were closed, locked, chained shut. What were they closed for? To keep him out? Probably. Not even the coffee shop would take his bits of change, either.

Touching his leg, feeling the bone, hard and rigid against the skin, he thought, *I'll close my eyes. Just for a minute. Tomorrow, I'll get it looked at. But a little rest first. Yeah, rest.*

Sleep came easy. Too easy.

His mind showed him pictures of the sea, vast and rolling and blue.

(Granddad's summer home? Vancouver Island. How old was I? Ten, twelve, maybe.)

He could hear it churning, as if it was going to give something up, an incessant beeping, reminding him of the chip-truck parking, kids running, pushing past one another to be first in line for Phantoms. He could hear voices, loud. Maybe they were vacationers, bawling at their children to get back from the waves, to wait for the truck to open shop? Was he in the water, too? Swimming? He could feel the weight of it around him, cooling him as he dove down. He held his breath. Suddenly, the water seemed to get heavy around him, the pressure dangerous somehow. He tried to hold his breath a few seconds more, to keep his lungs filled, to stay afloat, but he was scared, thought of drowning. His head felt pressurized, about to implode. He opened his mouth, felt the rush of water enter him and fill his lungs with heavy lead.

And then he felt nothing at all.

As he cocked the small rifle, a little piss-ant .22, the thunderous whoosh reminded the scraggly teenager of low-flying jets, mean thunderclouds. Dusk was coming on fast, the shadows long and dense, making it like night under here.

Content to smash beer bottles lined up on a plastic milk crate, he aimed, pulled the trigger, and heard a low pop, not much louder than a pellet gun would make, watched as the brown glass exploded.

"That's four," Darren said, handing Shaun the gun.

He cracked it over his knee, reloaded, pulled a flask out of his jacket and took a long pull. Gritting, blowing hot air out from his belly: "Move, I has a go."

Letting off a dozen rounds, two bottles went down, and that was it.

Darren laughed. "Jesus, mate, you *must* be pissed."

"Not like you, I'd say." He staggered to the crate, lined up another half-dozen at the bottom of the massive concrete pillar, which rose up sixty feet to meet the overpass.

Another rig drove by, booming around them. Shaun looked up, watched it pass.

"Ever go hunting?" Darren asked him.

They passed the flask around. "No. You?"

"Nope. I'm a townie, man. Sure I haven't even been past the city."

Shaun fixed his hat, let off a few more rounds. "I'm not worth shit at this. Let's get back to the house, and I'll get us a plate of something. I'm half-starved."

"Nothing else to be at, I suppose."

They started out across the empty lot, walking between oily puddles, broken glass, drooping bags of garbage. Gulls cawed and pecked at rotten food. Shaun took a pot shot at one, missed.

"What in the Christ are the two of you at?" someone called out from behind them, the slurred and rough voice echoing off the concrete, coming at them from all around.

They turned, unable to see anyone in the shadows.

Peering forward, Shaun said, "Who's that? And what's it to you what we're up to?"

A scabby figure stepped out, clutching at the concrete, a bottle in his other hand, almost polished. His eyes looked mad, blared out from behind his crusty face, dirty beard. Overcoat slung down around his shoulders, too big for his slight, starved frame, he tried to steady himself, stumbled forward. "This is my spot here. You get your own, you two little pricks."

They looked at each other, emitting either a laugh or a grunt. "Get a load of this old fool."

"Laugh at me, will you, hey?" he slurred, smashing the bottle against the concrete, brandishing the broken neck like a weapon, swinging it in a slashing motion. "I told you to get out. This... This is *my* spot, by Jesus!"

Darren nudged his buddy, took aim, fired.

The man squealed, fell over, gripped his left knee. "Oh, Christ, you've gone and busted me. I'll never walk right again—not *ever!*"

"What did you do that for?"

"Does it matter? That's the old fuck we see downtown all the time. Stinks of piss. Dad says they should throw them all in the funny farm."

Rolling in the dirt, the man let out another moan.

"Think he's really hurt?"

Feeling big, like a man: "Watch." Darren made a step forward and fired, sure that it'd found a home. Puffs of smoke trailed out from the short barrel, thinned, vanished, and they watched the man cry out again, hold himself. He was in a bad way.

"Let's get," Shaun said, worried.

Darren nodded, stuffed the rifle in his jacket.

They ran off.

He'd heard the pop of bottles, low, muffled, and the laughter: distant, dream-like. The high whine of the dog had roused him, the legless dog, unnamed, wrapped in a nest of newspapers at the bottom of a busted shopping cart. Peeling the soiled blanket back, staggering to his feet, his knees wanting to finally give up the good-fight, he'd taken a swig and rounded the corner. His vision was bad, like peering through smoke, fog, but he could make out two boys drinking a ways off, letting off shots. That's what he'd heard: shots. Didn't they know those were *his* bottles, that it was *his* lot? He'd had a few words, to send them off, then they'd put a few in him.

Feeling himself leak, he touched the dime-sized holes with his index finger: one in the right knee, another in the belly. "Dirty sods," he moaned, stuffing a wad of newspapers up his shirt.

The mutt yelped.

He looked at his hand, red and wet, steadied himself against the concrete pillar. Weak: "I'm done, boy. Finished."

Slumping back to the ground, he left a red handprint on the concrete.

Hauling the blanket across his legs, he felt a tremor go through him, heard a distant rumble like thunder clouds in the distance. Then the ground shook, as if to erupt beneath him. Bottles lined on the ground rattled and danced, the dog following them as they spun, whining. His makeshift tent—an ancient tarpaulin strung up on a rotten mop that was laid across two stacks of plastic milk cartons—made a staccato beat, tilted and collapsed. "What the Christ?"

A crack appeared between his legs, widened, looked like lightning. He rolled out of the way as it ran up the length of the pillar and split the concrete in a flash, reminding him of something from the Bible. A cloud of thick dust coughed out, stinking of rot, worse than even him. His eyes got wide, and he watched as a blackened hand shot out, reaching, clawing. The ground continued to shake, grew violent. The crack expanded and, like a breached uterus, opened up and spit out a body. The dusty figure lay there next to him, motionless, chest unmoving, face buried in the dirt.

Wanting out, the dog barked, bit at the cart, did scared circles on its bandaged stumps.

Sounding like the dog: "Oh, Jesus, it's a devil come up to get me!"

The heap of dirty clothes moved, shifted, lifted its head and pushed itself up. Turning, face a patchwork of parchment skin and bone, two black socket holes for eyes, its ragged hair, eyebrows, eyelashes caught in chunks and bits of concrete that dangled and weighed it down. It moaned something, sounding like wind through a gutter. His shirt, torn, hanging, rags, flapped, exposing xylophone ribs that were encased in a vault of grey.

The old man cried, more than still drunk and already halfway dead, "That's it. That's it. I'm done. Get it over with. I'm not worth much, anyhow." He could feel the blood and piss run out and watched it mix in a puddle beneath him.

Hauling itself up, the wraith of a man went to the dog, put out its hands, bone hands, and petted it, stroked its head. The mutt cowered back.

The old man, forgetting his fear, tried to get up, but fell back on his hole with a hard thud, screeching in pain. Arms outstretched, as in supplication: "Take me. Take me instead. He's done nothing, and I'm just some old prick."

Something whined out of the thing's throat, whistled. Grabbing a piece of broken plastic, it bent—knees creaking, hinges in need of an oiling—and it drew a rough sketch in the muddy ground: a box, slices aiming down on it, a stickman within the box, then a cross through the stickman. He—by the size of it, it'd surely been a *he*, the old wino figured—closed his hands around his throat, tight, choking, and pointed to the thick concrete pillar, to the fissure he'd poured out of, tapped it.

Through his drunk, the old man seemed to understand. White, little blood left in him, out of his mind and gripping his side: "Lord Christ, almighty! They drowned you in there, did they? Oh, Jesus. They talks about you, you know. I'm sure it's you. Just has to be you. Says you just up and left one day, never showed your face again. But I've heard yarns about you getting yourself killed when they were building this here overpass. Suppose that one is true, then. I should be thankful that I just got two in me, instead of what you got."

Hands out to warm against the fire, the flaps of its cheeks moved, exposing the hinge of its jaw.

The pool beneath the wino was now considerable. "I'm tired, my son. I don't got much left in me, I think. Me poor mutt. You'll see to him, won't you?"

Bone-hands gripped the wino's leg, nodded.

Even without eyes, just his black holes for eyes, he watched the old man heave two heavy breaths, go still for a moment, and he let out one last long, wheezing sigh. His eyes, wet, unblinking, stared off.

The dog yelped, stuck its snout in the air, sniffed, sensing death.

Poor bugger, Bone-hands thought, petting it, sitting by the fire with a heavy thud.

This place, the lot, once home, had changed very little. The landscape was flat and dirty, a patchwork of mud and crushed rock. Garbage was strewn about; ravenous gulls pecked at garbage bags that looked like half-deflated party balloons. The wooden box, his tomb, was gone, replaced by the concrete pillar. An overpass roared above him.

How long had he been buried within its bowels? A year, two, ten, twenty?

Were the men with hardhats still around, still violent, anxious to put their boots to his face? Maybe.

He felt his spine at the base of his neck, exposed, rigid, touched his mouth and watched his lips crumble away, looked down at this chest. How could he even feed himself? What nourishment could he possibly get, or need? Were the coffee shops and diners still open, still in existence?

He removed the wino's hat and coat, tattered scarf, hid his body in them, placed a soiled and wet blanket over the wino's breathless body.

Bone-hands scooped the dog up easily. His body creaked as he set out across the lot, mutt nestled tight under his arm. His body felt strong enough to snap and break without thinking—not weak, like before, weak from hunger and booze.

Its fur was tangled, wet, and it shivered violently, gut gurgling over with hunger. Bone-hands sensed this—something deep within him, something instinctive, primal, bubbling up from the bottom of his brain to the front of the consciousness. He could not feel it. No. He could not feel much, not much at all.

The streets were dead, quiet, cold, a wasteland of concrete and pavement, dim streetlamps. Little had changed. Downtown was still just rows of ugly, sulking, drooping houses, a block of brick and glass banks, bars. Paper cups and newspapers clogged the gutters; the skeletal framework of scaffolding ran the lengths of the shops, which were closed, silent, their faces black, black.

He walked the streets, his boots clunking, sounding like lead shoes on the sidewalks.

The dog cried with hunger.

Smashing through a glass display would be easy enough, but he couldn't be seen, caught, not like this. He searched through trashcans, sanitation dumpsters—all empty, a stinking grease lingering at the bottom.

His stomach, a dried pit encased in concrete, did not need nourishment. But he remembered hunger, like a hard beating, his death. The old man, drunk, devoid of much life, could do little for the dog but let it starve, its ribs as visible as his own, a wreck.

He went to the corner where he had begged. It stank of piss, vomit—still frequented by drunks. But it was late, deserted. The newspaper stand was still there, a sentry, plastered with peeling posters, screaming slogans and cover charges. Winter was hard, fast and mean, and with the wind ripping at him, like now, cutting through his clothes, summer clothes, layers upon layers of them, he used to press his back to it to escape the cold, waiting for the bars to let out, for the university crowd to spew forth. Dancing, singing, playing a harmonica, whatever kept them laughing, entertained, clapping their hands. A paper bag turned down to collect change is how he ate, drank, survived, lived.

Sunken, weak, dark eyes wet with hunger. That is how he remembered his own dog, Grey. The thought that this dog, much worse off, and now his own, pained him.

He could not see his breath. He had no breath; there was no need for him to breathe, being dead. But the dog's came out in icy, desperate pants.

People were generous in winter, pitying, especially women. They'd surely reach deep in their pockets for a legless dog, a starved mutt.

He was sure.

Chunks of concrete, grey dust fell from the harmonica—left in the folds of his jacket—as he tapped it off his boot. Cupping it, he put it to his mouth, his lips skillfully dancing on the silver, sending out puffs of dust, a rich buzz coming out over the whine of his throat.

The dog, covered in newspapers, cocked its head, puzzled. He was squeezed into a plastic grocery basket. Without his legs, he was light, easy to carry.

Bone-hands petted its head, rubbed its chin.

A freak show, he had to mask his appearance: eyes, face, hands. His reflection—twisted, misshapen in a dirty hubcap mirror—now reminded him of *The Invisible Man*. His esophagus, exposed, coral-like, was concealed by a roll of duck tape and a rotten scarf. His face was covered in a ski mask, black plastic sunglasses. His cheeks, flaps of skin blowing out as he exhaled into the harmonica, like linen in the wind, the teeth he still had on full display, had also been taped down beneath the mask.

Voice wheezing, sounding like an asthmatic: "I'll get you fed soon, my friend."

Two quarters and a crumpled drink ticket lay at the bottom of his paper bag—small, insignificant. He stared at them, thinking they'd multiplied in the few minutes since he'd last looked down.

There was little human traffic, even here, at his usual spot, his lucky spot. The bars hadn't let out yet, so there was still hope. They'd be good and pissed this time of night, generous. Sometimes, crowds would sing and dance around him in drunken reverie, and would empty their pockets eagerly. The next morning, amongst the coins and dollar bills, he'd find condoms, breath mints, tightly wrapped packets of weed.

There was no laughing now, only the dog crying, and the howl of the wind, like an angry wolf.

"Have some faith, boy," he said.

A series of laughs, cracked voices, came from down the street. He looked up, saw five men emerge from an alleyway. They staggered, held onto one another for support. Two of them had no jackets, their shirts flapping in the wind; they didn't seem to mind the bitter cold.

He looked at the dog. "This is what I was talking about now."

Tapping his foot in rhythm, he started playing, his lips running up and down the steel bridge skillfully, lungs working in short, hard, half-bursts. The name of the tune was lost to him. He'd picked it up in Bay de Verde. When, he couldn't remember.

"Christ, that's Bill Emberley, lads," one of the boys said, dancing a drunk dance, pirouetting. They were young, university students, all too obvious from their Hawaiian shirts and runners, gelled hair. "*Hard, Hard Times?*"

One of the others nudged Bone-hands, his words coming out slow like mud. "Is he right, or what?"

Bone-hands nodded, still playing.

"Alright!" He started singing, dancing around, the words all slurred and sluggish. *"The best thing to do is to work with a will. For when it's all over you're hauled on the hill."* He reached into his pocket, hauled out several bills, threw one in the paper bag. "That's just great, man. Wish there were more of you guys playing out here. There's too many fucks just sitting around, stinking of piss, begging. Hate it. At least you're fucking doing something."

One of his friends, irritated: "Man, don't give him any money. It just encourages them."

Another staggered out into the street, face white and wet with pearls of sweat, arms flailing, tried to hail a cab. "Man, I'm dying here. We have to go." Bone-hands watched him bend at the knees and empty his stomach out onto the road with a greasy splash. "Jesus, boys, come-the-fuck-on!"

"Yeah, wait another minute. It's your own goddamned fault you're polluted." He threw another dollar bill into the bag. "You know any others?"

Trying to hide the dry rasp of his voice, low: "Maybe." He started in on the only other song he knew from the Bay, the notes high, sharp, quick.

"Isn't anything I know. But not bad. Not bad."

Lurching, looking plague-ridden, the boy had come in off the street, abandoning any hope for a cab. His eyes were wide, angry, hands clenched into fists, grinding them into the hood of a Dodge. Leaning over the car, his chest rising, falling, slow: "One last time: come on. *Now!*"

"Jesus, will you—"

He shot forward, the others watching him move, caught in disbelief. Kicking the dog squarely in the stomach, sending it skidding across the sidewalk in a long yelp, he raised his hands high, brought them down in an axe-handle on the crown of Bone-hands' head. There was a distinct crack, and the boy cried in pain, sounding worse than the dog. He held up his hands—broken, looking like petrified and gnarled tree branches—and stared at them in disbelief. Slumping to his knees: "They're broke! Jesus, Jesus. They're fucking *shattered*."

Bone-hands stood up, looked at the dog. Quick puffs of shallow breath came out of it, tongue hanging out and limp on the concrete, its chest was surely crushed, smashed. If it was, he wouldn't last long, not long at all.

Pointing at the animal: "You killed my dog. *My* dog."

(*Me poor mutt. You'll see to him, won't you?*)

Despite his heavy, concrete limbs, he was quick, quicker than the boys, backhanding one of them. His head—for Bone-hands it was a soft head, like tissue—snapped to the side, and there was a crack and distinct pop as his left eye became pulp and his face a mashed mess, which was left with a deep and horrible impression of a fist. He then hit the brick wall and bounced off, falling in a dead heap. The other one ran down the sidewalk, arms flapping. Bone-hands threw his harmonica, hitting the boy squarely in the back of the skull, where it stayed, sticking out like it'd always been part of his skull. He went down face-first onto the concrete, twitching.

Still staring at his broken hands, pissing himself: "Please, mister. Just leave me. I'm sorry. I... I didn't know what I was doing. I got carried away."

Bone-hands looked at the dog, its eyes wide, staring, skin like a thin shawl over its ribs. He touched its ribs; they were not broken. It would live. "That Country Chicken plant still down around here somewhere?" he asked the boy.

"Mister, just let me go. Please, I won't say anything. Christ, I swear. I'll say I got into some fight, or something. There's always all kinds down here. No one will know. Oh, Jesus, let me go."

Kicking him in the ribs, the crack distinct over the scream: "Is it?"

Holding his side: "Yeah... Yeah, sure, but it's closed long ago. It's—"

Bone-hands grabbed him by the ears, pushed his head to the cement, put his knee to the boy's face and pressed down. There was a soft crunch and a mucous snort as his face collapsed, sounding like a garbage compactor, and his blood and brain tissue spilled out across the sidewalk as Bone-hands ground his skull down into pulp.

Scooping him up over his shoulder, Bone-hands put the dog in his basket, leaving the others where they were, to bleed out and freeze onto the sidewalk, to be found later by the sanitation crews that came around at first light to clean up messes on the sidewalks.

It was a derelict building. The windows were black, cracked, the whole structure covered in the same copper grime of rust and decay. Half-gutted by fire, the right side lay exposed, a wide staircase winding, leading to nowhere. Large culverts led down to a river where waste, the unusable parts of the carcass—thick, bloody slop and beaks and claws—had been disposed of and sent out to sea.

Hunched, the concrete of his limbs grinding with each step, he went in through one of these culverts, a death tunnel, carrying the dog and the body of the dead boy. It opened up into an empty vat, the steel walls high, a ladder leading out of it. The floor was a rusted out blade, used to cut and dice and divide before it was pumped out into the river. The place stank of rotten meat and mildew and salt and bloody chicken parts. He imagined it was a stench that would never leave—it was part of the place now, like a soul. Climbing out, dark machines stood like large, mysterious, vicious beasts, curling towards the ceiling, reaching out, stretching the length of the place.

The dog whined.

"You'll be good soon, buddy. Promise," he told the dog.

Feeling his way through, he quickly found what he'd come for, a stained bucket left beneath it. Screwed into a grey chopping block, thick with rust, he turned the crank, a long screech of pain coming out of it, echoing. It would do.

Stripping the boy, leaving his clothes in a pile, he fed him, legs first, into the yawning maw of the grinder, the rest of him lying lengthways on the chipped chopping block. Slowly going down, inch by inch, forcing him down, stuffing him in, his bones snapping under the pressure of pulverizing, grinding metal, coming out the other end in strings of bloody meat. He could see bits of bone, nail, skin, in with the meat, now mincemeat, which slopped down into the bucket, quickly filling it to the brim.

The dog stirred; its snout twitched, sniffed at the air, and it licked its lips.

"Enough here for weeks, buddy," Bone-hands said, stuffing and grinding, wondering where he could cook it up to and then store the leftovers. "We'll stay here. The rest of the winter won't be too bad for us."

Home Is Where the Heart Is

"**I** couldn't find a damn thing; the store was picked clean. I don't know what we're going to do, baby. I just don't know. Jesus in heaven, why? That prick Nagin should've had us gone days ago."

Gerald was out on the bedroom windowsill, his head buried deep between his legs, his paint-stained hands clutching greasy hair. The lines of his face were cut deep with anxiety, and he looked older, as if he had aged ten years in the last few days.

Maggie had never seen her husband cry, not ever. He was concrete. Half a lifetime in the Army had done that to him. Seeing her man like this made her feel weak, empty, like a dark hole was spreading out across her chest and swallowing her.

She put her arms around him, kissed his neck. "Baby, we'll find your mother something. Don't worry," she said, glad that he couldn't see her face. "Someone will get to us soon. You'll see. They can't miss the sign."

Black oily water was up to the top of the stairs. After the levee along the 17th Street Canal had burst, neighborhoods had quickly become submerged. The main roads were a river of garbage and human waste. Rats and snakes were everywhere. Every so often, a body would float past clutching at a makeshift raft. They lost count just how many. Dozens, maybe.

Even the gun blasts had stopped. They had been constant at first, when the roads had been congested with parades of madness and people had been scared out of their minds, fleeing their homes, animal cages and luggage in tow. Police had been everywhere, brandishing automatic weapons, unafraid to fire. Looking for batteries, kerosene, whatever he could find, Gerald actually saw people trying on clothes in broken display windows of stores: dresses, hats, coats.

The city had become a nuthouse.

A few, the very last stragglers, living in single-level homes, were forced to blast their way to the roof to be plucked up by Chinooks.

But things were silent now, like night. No animals. No people.

The water churned and rushed past, a dark, dangerous river that had grown into a new polluted sea.

At the outset, Gerald had insisted on staying. That had been stupid; he knew that now.

That had been days ago, before his mother had run out of insulin and they had started feeding her spoonfuls of sugar. Now she was in a semi-coma, her breath low and ragged. If Gerald could find insulin, she might live. The radio said that there was a triage center at the Armstrong Airport, but there was no way to get her there. Maybe Chalmette High, where the OEP had set up shop.

Maggie kept thinking of the man on the radio who had lost his wife after they had managed to chop a hole in the roof with an axe. *I was holding her hand as tight as I could, and she told me to take care of the kids. Then she slipped from my grip.* Maggie wished and prayed for the screeching bullhorn to return. It was unlikely. The radio said they hadn't evacuated the Superdome yet. Hearing what people were going through over there—thousands living in their own

waste, the dead lying around with no one to remove them—
made her feel sick, weary, abandoned.

"Have you tried the houses up the street? The
McGoverns'?" she asked him, hoping to give him hope.
They were old, like Gerald's mother. "Didn't they say they
were staying?" They had money, two cars. There hadn't
been anything to keep them here. But some people were
staying. Their houses a hundred years old, they talked about
being *true* New Orleanians and weathering the storm.

"I'm not sure," he said. "It's getting dark. I'll have to
wait until tomorrow morning. I just hope Mom can hold
on."

The woman was in her seventies; she was lucky to have
lasted this long. "She will. She's strong."

For an hour, they watched over her and talked.
Maggie, the eternal optimist, spoke of rebuilding: things
could be good again, like on the base. They just had to
persevere.

A dog barked in the distance, then another, then still
more, echoing between the houses.

Gerald got up. "Christ, where is it coming from?" He
couldn't see anything. The streetlamps had gone dead two
days ago, and stood like dark totems.

Maggie got the flashlight. "There!" she said, pointing.

Scanning the river, there were a dozen dogs swimming
upriver, a few floating on an old mattress, the rest trying
frantically to stay above water.

"Where did they all come from?" she asked.

"SPCA must've let them out before they got flooded.
Better than having them drown in cages."

One was about twenty feet out, and she spotlighted it,
its eyes wide and frantic, icy air coming out of its snout in
short, quick, exhausted breaths. "Look at their faces,
Gerald. They're terrified."

"Might be swimming from the rats. Animals can sense
disease."

They watched in silence, the only sound water splashing, the river surging.

Pointing: "Oh, Jesus! Did you see that?"

"What?"

"There! There it is again!"

"Where? Where?"

He grabbed her by the shirt and pointed. "There, two of them just plopped under like something grabbed them from beneath."

"What grabbed them? Maybe they just couldn't keep going."

"No! Jesus, I saw it. They were swimming and then just went under—no struggling. One second they were there, the next gone."

Maggie whistled, calling the dogs.

"Shut up! We can't have them here. Who knows what they got?"

Two more went under, yanked from below the surface, their yelps cut off in mid-breath.

They both saw it. "Jesus..." she moaned.

Gerald took the rifle from against the dresser and fired two shots into the water. His chest heaving, he waited, watched, not knowing if it would do any good, if there was even anything to hit at all.

Another dog went under. Gerald let off a salvo this time, blasting their ears, and expending the rest of the cartridges, the air pungent with cordite.

They waited, Maggie gripping her sides and scared witless, expecting to see more of them go under, but the water had gone calm again. The rest of the dogs kept swimming.

The night had been oppressively hot and balmy, making the air feel like it was sticking to the walls of your lungs, choking your brain.

Maggie had dreamt of the water drowning them in their sleep, coming up over the stairs, carrying rats and plague, flooding their bedroom.

Tied to the radiator just below the window, the boat had been knocking against the outside paneling low and dull, which had woken them.

They had turned on the radio to hear the latest evacuation reports. Things were bleak. Aaron Broussard, President of Jefferson Parish, gave an interview for some news program, sobbed uncontrollably, talked about the mother of the guy who ran the building he was holding up in. She had been stuck in a nursing home, unable to be rescued. Day after day, her son had promised to send help. He was unable, and she had drowned. *Nobody's coming to get us. Nobody's coming to get us.*

Gerald had switched it off. It was nothing they needed to hear.

Sitting on the edge of the bed, rifle between his legs, Maggie in the doorway, he started talking about Iraq. "I still think of Lieutenant Rodriguez a lot, but mostly nights. The image that I have is him with most of his chin and jaw blasted away, trying to speak."

"Baby..." Maggie started, putting her hands on his shoulders.

"I saw some crazy fucking shit after that. Shit they would never dare show on the news. It never got in my head and stayed like that did." He stopped for a moment, wiped the sweat off his face, both of them drowning in sweat. He had already decided on some things: "The way I figure it, Mama might already be gone. But there's a slim bit of hope. I have to try. We owe her that much."

Gerald loaded the rifle, took a black Magic Marker and wrote their Social Security Numbers on their forearms. "Just in case either of us get, you know, drowned. We have to be practical about this."

After that, he went out.

It was noon now; he would be back soon.

Maggie was with his mother, holding her hand. Her breathing was lower than ever, her lips so blue you would swear she was already dead. She was mumbling things: fevered dream talk. Sometimes Maggie could make some sense out of it, most times not.

She was on the brink. Even if a rescue team swooped down, it might already be too late. Maggie had seen some of the elderly on the television before the electricity had gone out, tired and sick and weak. They were huddled together out in front of the Superdome, stretched out on lawn chairs, frying under the fat, blazing sun. There were even reports of rapes and beatings. They all had an unforgettable expression carved into their faces: *We've been saved, but what now?*

"When he gets back, it'll be all fine," she told his mother, staring at the thick black numbers he had slashed on her forearm, doubting herself. "You'll see. It'll be all fine."

Two blocks up, the McGoverns' was like a time capsule. Beds were made, the plush white carpet clean and vacuumed. A basket of fresh laundry sat in the hallway, waiting to be put away. Even the curtains—stiff, long and white—had been recently starched. The bathroom had been scrubbed clean and bleached, too. Going through the medicine cabinet—empty—Gerald could almost see his reflection in the sink. The maid had been busy right up until the end. There were even air fresheners in every room, but he could still smell the river flowing below him: rot and human waste, erasing their memories and lives, their past and future.

This was the last house on the street. Crocker's Convenience was completely submerged next door. There was a 7-Eleven a few blocks up, but there wouldn't be much left. On CNN, video footage showed hordes of people scurrying out of other stores with loads of goods in their hands, police standing by helpless, watching.

Gerald got in the boat. They would just have to hold up, wait. *Can't be much longer*, he figured, ripping the cord. The Louisiana National Guard was making trips neighborhood by neighborhood. It was only a matter of time. *Another day, maybe two. Mama will hold on. She got to.*

"*Gerald!*" someone called out. With the water rushing, the voice sounded far and distant. "What are you doing in my house, man?"

He threw himself around.

There, standing on the façade of a duplex across the street, waist deep in water, was Mitchell McGovern.

"Christ, what are you doing over there?"

"There's a bunch of us. We've got a generator and hot food. Get Maggie and your mother. Bring them over."

"Mama's sick. I can't move her. Do you have any medicine over there? Insulin? She's real sick, Mitchell."

"Of course, my friend. Come over, and we'll see what we can do."

Mitchell McGovern stood there staring, waiting, a permanent smile slit across his face, his arms tight at his sides, his back straight. Gerald could see the old man's face was ashen, his clothes soaking wet, his gray hair pasted to his head, like he had taken a dive into the river. Behind him, the windows of the house were closed: dark eyes.

Gerald let the motor die down, but kept it running. He had to be careful. Five policemen had been killed by sniper fire, a dozen more injured. A lot of people had lost it, sane people. And he knew that when faced with extinction, normal people could do some awful fucking things to one another.

"Why's the house so dark, Mitchell?" he asked, slowly reaching for the rifle at the bottom of the boat. "Anything wrong?"

"Nothing. Don't be foolish. Come over and get some hot soup into you."

There was something about his smile: forced, unnatural, imitated, a liar's smile. Gerald slowly raised the shotgun. "What's going on, Mitchell? Why are the windows dark? And why are you out in the water?"

The fiberglass hull knocked something, and Gerald looked over the side: the streets were littered with abandoned school buses. But something dark churned and slithered down there that looked like eels. They had come in from the sea, and the water was teeming with them.

There was a splash. He looked up. McGovern was gone, and the water rippled and bubbled where he had just stood.

Gerald wasn't chancing it. And thinking of the dogs, he revved the motor and swung the boat around fast.

Something hit the hull again, hard this time, and the boat tipped to the port side. Water poured in and sloshed around. Gerald lost his footing, and the gun fell out of his grip and plopped into the river. Desperate, he reached into the water, and something slick slid across his skin. Pain, sharp and stabbing, shot up his arm and across his chest, webbing out. Reeling back, a twisting pattern of tiny pink sucker marks curled up around his arm in a neat pattern, drawing blood.

The dark water suddenly got violent, foaming and spitting, shaking and tipping the boat dangerously, dipping beneath the surface, quickly filling it.

Gerald grabbed the sides.

Something pushed up from beneath. Then the boat was lifted from the bow and hauled at with a tremendous force. It dipped and stood almost straight up. Something was dragging him down, and the image of the dogs pulsed in his mind like a hazard light. Gerald pushed at the seats, tried to hold tight. For a second, he thought he saw Mitchell, swimming around a few feet below, his movements fluid, like an invertebrate.

The boat thrashed to the side violently. The fiberglass was wet, slippery, and he couldn't hold on, lost his purchase and belly-flopped forward, the cold polluted water quickly swallowing him. Then the boat tipped forward, came down on him like a ton, breaking his back, sending him to the pavement below.

Anxious, scared, Maggie sat on the ledge of the window, waiting for her man. The day had cooled and night was starting to descend. A few times, she had closed her eyes, listened to the water, and pretended she was off somewhere, back in Iowa. It was the banks of the Mississippi, maybe. That lasted for a moment until the wind picked up and the smell of shit and garbage blew past her, breaking the spell.

Gerald had been gone for the whole day now. In the half-light, she saw pieces of debris float by. Her heart would sink, thinking it was the boat, capsized, then what was left of the light would reveal it: some bit of metal or plastic, not Gerald and the boat. Then she would start in on another cigarette and tell herself he would be back soon.

So many times before, he had gone off and then come back days later—crazy, in a fit of depression and rage, thinking he was being followed by unknown forces—and he'd be back this time, too.

His mother was dead, had died in her sleep, just slipped away, quiet, and that worried her most. Her hands and feet and face were all blown out and purple. The swelling had even swallowed her eyes. To her, it was strange now, someone dying like that. She had begun to associate noise with death: screeching, gagging, choking.

They couldn't leave her in the back room. With all the heat, it wouldn't be long before she'd start to decompose.

And with the rats, there was disease to think about: plague, cholera, typhus. The water was teeming with them, squeaking and squealing, starved. There were even more of them within the last hour, hundreds. They were so thick in parts—patches of dirty gray and brown—that it looked as though you could walk right across their backs.

Gerald had the rifle. He was cautious, but she still worried.

She stood inside with the window closed, watching.

On all day yesterday, hoping to hear some specifics about some kind of help, there wasn't much juice left in the radio.

She flicked it on for a moment. It was President Bush again:

Mandatory evacuations have been ordered for New Orleans and Galveston. I urge the citizens to listen carefully to the instructions provided by state and local authorities. And follow them. We need you, the citizens, to be the first line of defense, to care for your neighbors and your community. To do your job, actively look for those in need of assistance.

She gave a disheartened laugh and lit another cigarette. Her throat was raw.

She turned off the radio.

Quiet.

The rats had stopped.

She got up and went to the window. They were gone, as if a wave had come and erased them.

Peering out, something slapped against the siding below. Startled, Maggie looked. Thick, a fat snake, maybe, something slid through the water.

She reeled back.

For a brief second, it reached up, a dark and thick shadow. Searching, it curled, whipped and snapped in front of the window, then receded back down.

(*No snake. Too big!*)

Clutching at her mouth, shaking, thinking of her husband: "Gerald..." His name trailed off.

The storm had left them with nothing. It'd left the whole city with nothing, forcing them to feed on one another. Whatever was in the water, having come in from the sea, having been swept inland, wasn't all that much different from them. It was desperate, she knew. Hungry.

She had handled the two trips to the VA in Crescent City, even gotten them through the time she found Gerald in the back room biting down on the barrel of his rifle before his mother had taken them in and they had moved to the city. She had done all that and she could do this; she had to do this.

With a pillowcase around her mouth and nose, she wrapped the old woman in her soiled bed sheets, dragged her out by the legs, and tied one of Gerald's dumbbells to her ankle, put her in the water.

She watched her slip into the darkness, her long white hair swaying like seaweed, hoping the thing would have her and then leave for good, and let them continue on.

Maggie dreamt of fishing, the low hum of their boat steady. Gerald was standing in it close to shore, hauling in a net brimming with silver trout, his arms tight and muscular and tanned. She dug her toes into the warm sand.

The sun was high and wide. A radio played something familiar.

Suddenly, the sky went dark, like a switch had been thrown. Cold sleet rained down and burned her bare skin. The water got violent and quickly rose past her knees until she was wading up to her hips. Something cold and slimy wriggled between her legs, brushed her skin. She could barely see Gerald, but she could see his eyes, bright like the moon.

Then she woke. It was still night. *What time?* She couldn't tell. *Four. Possibly later.*

She'd fallen asleep with the radio going. *Stupid! Goddamned stupid!* She turned the dial and tried the power. Nothing; not even fuzz. It was dead. *Stupid-fucking-shit!*

"Maggie, baby! Are you in there?"

Gerald! He was home.

She jumped to the window.

He was out in the river, standing in the boat, the motor silent. "I let the current carry me back," he said. "No gas left."

Crying, laughing: "Baby! You're alright then? Right?"

"Sure, I'm alright. But can you swim out? We have to get out of here."

"Gerald, it's still in the water: what got the dogs. It's in there, waiting. I saw it, Gerald. *I saw it!*"

He was smiling, but his eyes looked like he was staring at something dark and terrible a few feet in front of him. "Who knows when help's coming? Just come on. We'll find somewhere better, someplace safe. You'll be alright. C'mon. It's alright."

Maggie stepped back, waves of confusion consuming her. He hadn't asked about his mother. Maybe he had lost it. Maybe the old Gerald and his burdensome past, like an oppressive shadow, had reared its ugly head, sending him over the edge. "Gerald, are you okay?"

"Sure. Why?"

Her voice low and flat: "Your mother... She's gone, Gerald. She's gone..."

"You have to come on now, baby."

"Gerald, I had to put her in the river," she said, crying. "With you gone, I... I couldn't think of anything else."

"*Just come on, woman!*" The last word was like an accusation.

"Gerald?" Peering forward, she thought his face looked like a mask, dead skin. He was sick. He might even have yellow fever, like the radio talked about. She had to calm him, get his mind working straight. "Come back to the house, baby. You're sick. I'll throw you something to paddle over with."

She wrenched a shelf from the wall. Photo frames crashed to the floor.

There was a splash, and she turned. Gerald was gone.

She was at the window, screaming his name, thinking of what was in the water. "Gerald! *Gerald!*"

Silence—just the sound of the rushing water.

The batteries in the flashlight were low, the light faint. The beam barely reached out.

"Gerald! Gerald..." She slumped to the floor, crying, slamming the flashlight against the window ledge, smashing it to bits. She was scared, confused, helpless: a child.

Water splashed again. Like oil, she could barely see into the water. For a second, a brief moment, she thought she saw his face, white, gliding past at an unnatural speed.

"Oh, Jesus. Gerald."

Maggie dove into the water.

A few feet down, something nudged against her. She spun.

(*Gerald, where are you? God, where?*)

A minute passed: eternity. Scanning, grabbing, her lungs were about to burst. She had to get air.

She went up, and something slapped her thigh. She looked down and saw Gerald's face, pale like before, expressionless, lifeless, his body curled like a snake around her leg. She thrashed and screamed soundlessly beneath the water, taking large gulps into her lungs, beating him with her fists.

Without oxygen, her body quickly went heavy and weak.

Flashes of brilliant white were in her eyes. She blinked, and for a moment, she saw something else down below, something large and snake-like moving, writhing in a thousand directions, seemingly independent of one another. And a nest of eels with a hundred eyes, like a ball of knots, blinked simultaneously.

She could see the moon above her, murky, swaying. Reaching for it, Maggie took one last gulp from the river.

"Hello? Is there anyone left here?" Sgt. Lachica called out over the bullhorn. They had cut the engine, cruised down the street. "This is the Louisiana National Guard. We are here to evacuate you. *Hello?*"

There was no one left. The place was waterlogged, a ghost town. Everyone had already been evacuated or had gotten the good sense to leave before things had gone to shit.

"Sergeant, look over there," Private Hendrickson said.

Spray painted on the side of one of the houses was *HELP! PEOPLE HERE!*

Inside, the place was littered with dirty linen and garbage and stank of human waste. Rats scurried about.

"You know," the sergeant started again, staring into the back room, "I'll never understand, after they were told to leave, why so many people stayed. What were they going to save, anyway?"

They had been at the Jackson Barracks when the levees were breached, flood waters quickly covering cars and high-water trucks, trapping boats inside the armory, people rushing around in waist-deep water, trying to save equipment. After just twenty minutes, the water had risen fifteen feet.

The private rifled through a dresser. There were pictures of a couple on it, smiling, standing on a beach by a lake. "Guess they felt this was their home, that they belonged here."

Cold Deck

Utterly done in, everything ached. Francis sat at the small square dinner table heavily, the crisp fall air following him into the kitchen from outside like a familiar guest, a neighbor, carrying with it the smell of exhaust and woodchips. "What have you got on?" he asked his wife, June, putting his oily saws up on the linoleum placemat—she'd curse him royally if he stained her tablecloth.

Facing the sink, she washed her hands, dried them in her apron. She said, turning, "Vegetables and salt-beef. There's a bread pudding put up to have with your tea."

She brought him his supper, fed him. Watching his jaw chew in slow, deliberate movements, his eyes flat like dull light bulbs: "My son, what's wrong? You look bothered."

A deep sigh came up from the bottom of his gut. "They've closed her down."

"Closed what down?"

"Everything, maid. Everything. We'll be put out before the winter."

"Oh, Jesus. Oh, Jesus." She got up from the table, holding her face in her hands, pacing in tight circles. "We're done in then, Francis."

Staring at his saws, he hated them, wanted them smashed. He wished that inside the greasy yellow boxes, at the part where the metal latches clasped tightly around his wrists, that he had hands again, that he'd never given them up to begin with. "They called us into the shed first thing and told us. The company's hauling up to Labrador. Didn't say why, just that we're finished up. Cheaper up there, I suppose, like everything. They're taking it all with them, too, everything—even the harbor. They're leaving us bare."

June took several small splits from the dusty wood-box and fed them to the stove, watched them get eaten up, transfixed. As if she'd forgotten everything else: "We're done, my son."

"We'll have to move down around the cape, somewhere in town, maybe. That's all I can see."

She gasped. "What, the house?"

"A few of the boys were saying that's best. Haul her up and put her on a barge. Who can afford to start up new here? Not us, by Christ. I'm too old for that. And even if we do stay, there won't be a soul left."

"They can't do it. They can't. It's criminal, Francis. Criminal. But thank Jesus we got no youngsters..."

He looked at his arms. Thick and muscled, veins snaking over tight skin, larger than the rest of him, they ached from lugging his saws around. "I can't go blaming them now."

For a moment, they were quiet and listened to the wind wail and rip at the storm door, the aluminum frame rattling.

In one smooth motion, Francis undid the latches, slid his arms out from inside the saws and unhooked the cords using his teeth. He got up and placed them on the porch mat. His calloused stumps were sore. Several new blisters had formed, which were filled with fluid and ready to burst; they never did heal right. But June would soak and bandage them later, like always.

"There's a meeting down at the club the night after next. A few of the lads said a man from the government will be there to talk resettlement. Are we going?"

He noticed she seemed to be sinking down into the linoleum canvas of the floor, her knit sweater bunching up around the shoulders. "Better than not going, I suppose."

"Get us a cup of tea then, maid. I'm worn down from the goings on."

The bar was filled with stale cigarette smoke, dour and desperate faces. Hard, stern eyes stared up towards the company men and the government representative lined up at the front like the Last Supper.

"We wish that there were positions for you in Labrador," the short bald man said, seated to the far left, his voice squeaking, nervous. He was sweating, too, carefully adjusting his glasses every few seconds with his thumb and forefinger. "But I'm afraid that just isn't possible. However, the severance package we're offering you, we feel, is fair."

The government man to his right, small in his cheap tweed jacket, hair uncut around the ears, nodded.

The town barked in disgust, loud and raucous. Tools shot forward accusatorily—saws, clamps, drills—slammed down, rattling beer glasses, sending some to the thin and worn carpet that was dotted with salt-stains.

Standing, waving his arms to hush the crowd, the mayor said, "Keep her down, boys, and let the man speak. You'll get your chance."

Knit hat gripped tightly in his fist—one of the few fists still left in the town—choking the life from the hat, one of the older men stood up, beating it off the edge of the table every few words, like an exclamation point. "Lord Christ, you've left us to the sharks."

"Please, calm down, sir," the small government man said, rubbing his hairy nose.

"We'll be a town of paupers and rags! And what are some of us going to feed our youngsters with, hey? I'm sure yours will have their bellies full, though, won't they? *Won't they!*" His wife, frail and wrinkled, looking beaten, defeated, sat him down.

"And with the harbor," coughing, Hairy-nose started, staring at his hands, as if they held some answer as they danced with one another on the table, "although the company *will* move it north, the government has already begun plans to replace it within the next five years."

Someone shouted something unintelligible from the back of the bar, high, piercing, slurred: drunk-talk. The crowd turned, hushed for a moment. A man with cant hooks for hands, arms around his wife's shoulders, leering side to side, snorted. "That there's the nail in our coffin. We've got no chance. None. God knows the souls of men, sir, and yours is a goddamned rocky one."

Francis was there in the far-right corner, listening, heart sinking, taking long draws from his cigarette, bringing the smoke deep into his lungs, letting the ashes fall to his lap. "You think we'll be left here in five years? There won't be a dog on the streets in five years. And even if we did stay, eh, who's going to haul in what we need to get by? No one from the city, I tell you that. It won't be worth their time; too expensive. If they can't bring it up the bay, like that man said, we're done in."

The men at the front listened, shifting their feet and hands in a nervous two-step.

Francis held up his saws. His voice shook. "So this is all for nothing then, is it? Tell me it's for *something*."

June, next to him, touched his leg. *Poor man. Can he even remember what it was like to have hands? Can he remember what they looked like, how to even use them?*

"And it's not just me," Francis continued, eyes wet. "The whole town gave up a hell of a lot to keep you running. Now all we get is a kick in the hole. You're thieves, simple as that!"

Applause roared through the small bar.

As if passing sentence, the five men rose, pushed their chairs in and put on their coats. They wanted out, fast, before things got ugly, confused. "On behalf of the company, we'd like to offer our sincere thanks. Over the years, you've all been model—"

"Sincere thanks, eh? *Eh!*" Winny Murphy, old and back-bent, arms and legs crooked with arthritis, on her feet, her toothless mouth slid into a gummy, hate-filled snarl. "You see these?" She held up a pair of gray, worn spikes, dirty, the leather mottled, soles cracked, white fiberglass prosthetics still attached, rusted buckles hanging like umbilical cords where they had once been attached to a knee. "They were my mister's. You poisoned him, you did. He had them for less than a year then did away with himself. I got nothing—same as they'll get."

She threw them towards the front, hideous things, looking like real legs, legs severed at the knee.

The crowd gasped.

Hairy-nose turned away, hands covering his eyes.

Winny started to the front, gripping chairs for support. "Here, they're poison, like the company." She turned to the crowd. "And you know what you're supposed to do with poison, eh? Cut it out. Too late for that, though. It's too late."

The party line was buzzing, the operators dizzy with reconnects. Two-hour waits for outgoing calls. Nothing could get in from the city.

Conversations were filled with venom and hate, but no tears. The women of the town, the wives, they were past that.

An open line. Two of them on: June and her cousin's wife, Maud.

"He's already at it. He'll be sat at that television staring at his saws. Pains the nerves. I feel right helpless."

June was tired, and the skin around her eyes looked like deep bruises. She wanted to sleep hours ago, her future, *their* future, a dark and oppressive burden.

"Frank's the same," Maud said. Her husband had agreed to let them have his legs. The decision haunted them regularly. "I'll find him out there in the shed with the bottle to his head almost polished off. He's too proud to drink in the house."

Voice cracking, June: "We'll all be finished soon enough, sure. They'll have the haulers in at the harbor in a few days; lumber's already gone. Only a matter of time, now. Last ship with supplies is due in Tuesday, I heard. Have they come up with something else?"

"Truck will be in once a month, not every other week."

"Times will be tight, girl."

June: "Tight, yeah..." She had watched the news and had seen the segment on them. Audio inserts insinuating a mild contempt for the small community, like what they were left with was a blessing, a sacrament: *the Lord giveth, and the Lord taketh away.* The reporter was from the outports, accent bleached. "Wouldn't know now, but we were all sitting home, waiting for our checks. That's the way the crowd in town likes to see it." Lately, she kept revisiting her mother's death in her head, something she hadn't done since her adolescence. She'd dreamt it, accompanied by a soundtrack of screaming. Her mother's splayed legs, midwife hunched down between them, blood reaching up past her elbows. Other women standing around the kitchen clutching at each other, their faces stiff with concern. Standing in the doorway, June, a child, watched between their legs, anxious to see her new brother, or sister. Then the baby was free, covered in blood and bits of membrane, but limp and quiet—*so still*—her mother pushing out the placenta, crying mad for her baby. Fast forward. Then her mother was still, head tilted to the side, staring, eyes wide and vacant. The midwife had something wrapped in a clean blanket, something small. She said something, something about the doctor. The doctor was away, in town, and unable to come. *But he knew she'd be ready any day.* It was at that point that she woke, disoriented, confused, angry. Filled with anger.

Maud: "Heard there's a bonfire planned. Mister's been going on about it."

"Where? I haven't heard nothing from Francis."

"The boys, they're burning their tools," she said, hoping that as they watched the fleshy plastic blacken, twist and melt, they'd all find their true selves again. "But I don't think much good will come out of it."

"Neither do I, maid."

"They should take their tools to that barge, before the job gets done."

"Yes, take them to something, I'd say."

For a moment, a silence came over the line, the faint white hum of static.

"The three of them down to the club to start with," June said contemptuously. "By Christ, be done with the whole lot."

The house was quiet: radio off, small television on the counter muted, news anchor mouthing the weather. An empty flask of rye was left on the table, a drop unfinished, left in the glass next to it. The heat was turned down. She touched the wood stove: cold, unlit, probably dead for hours. "Francis?" June called out. Her voice echoed.

No response.

He was asleep, up in bed, surely. "Francis?"

In the living room, two small patches of oil were on either side of his recliner, which looked like black holes. He'd been sitting there, drinking, his saws leaking drips onto the floor.

Anxiety began to creep out from her gut in webs.

She went upstairs. Frost had collected on the windows, thick. She could see her breath, icy.

The bed was made, not slept in, the blankets still tight and tucked beneath the mattress.

"*Francis?*" she yelled.

The rough cough of his saws choking to life came from outside, in the shed. It sounded like he couldn't haul on the cords, too drunk, too sluggish to snap them out from his hips where they were attached at his belt. Then a loud buzzing roar ripped through the house as they came to life, hungry animals.

June dashed down the stairs.

Accidents were not unknown to him, and his leathery arms were roadmaps of ragged scars and skin grafts. He was clumsy when he drank, thought he still had hands, thought he was still a young man and the saws were some dream, some unreality.

The shed door was open, smoke billowing out in a greasy trail of iron grey, stinking of exhaust.

"Francis, *Jesus!*" At that moment, the image of her father came to her, that image of meeting him at the harbor when he came home from Europe, dirty and tired from two weeks at sea, skinny, wasted, and sick from a bout of influenza. His face looked slack, dark, shadows hiding in the lines around his eyes and mouth. She'd barely recognized him. He'd died later that year, from a broken heart, not from the influenza. The war had never left him.

That was her husband: defeated.

Francis was on the large stump he cut junks on, tiny flecks of vomit clinging to his beard. Drunk, his arms were crisscrossed, swaying some, elbows resting on his lap and about to bring the spinning metal teeth down on his wrists, to do away with himself, to have it all over with.

She grabbed him by the shoulder. "My son, what in the name of Christ are you at? *What?*"

Head low, too low: "I'm not worth much. Not much at all. Best leave me to it. You'll be better off."

She slapped him, hard, jerking his head to the side.

Ashamed, he looked up at her.

And that was it for her—the look, not the slap. It was a look no man should ever have, a look reserved for widows. It made her feel weak, abused.

The saws slowed, gurgled once, twice, and coughed out. Francis undid the latches. Between the tools he could no longer use—hammer, bench saw, level—two large hooks were nailed high above his chipped workbench, beneath them dark and distinct shapes, like A-bomb flash burns on the sidewalk. He hung up his saws. "They're there for good now, my dear," he mumbled.

"Good thing," she sighed, wrapping her arms around his thick, square shoulders. "It's been too much for you lately. Go in the house and sit down, and I'll fix you a plate of something. We'll watch the news."

"I've got that to go to tonight, down the cove. I don't want to be going. But they all look up to me."

He saw something in her eyes that wasn't there before, ever—*hatred, maybe...?*—like a skinny, devilish beast, lurking, starved. "Yes, you'd best. It'll be good for you."

The fog had come in, swallowing faces, erasing features, blotting out the sky, the sun—sea fog, thick and soupy, the color of dirty silver dollars, smelled and tasted of saltwater. Two dozen men were there, all loggers, men with tight, dour faces with coarse beards and shaggy eyebrows that curved down in consternation, stoking-caps that were smeared with the grease of work. Standing around in a semicircle, some in wheelchairs, on crutches, others with no arms or hands, like Francis, they piled their tools—their limbs—and doused them with gasoline. It was a large pile, a heap of fiberglass and metal latches, steel teeth and hooks, arms and legs poking out.

The harbor, behind them, down past the grassy bluff and over the short cliff, growled and churned. The wind had come in, bringing ocean spray. The fog carried sounds, too: machines taking the harbor, placing the dismantled pieces on barges. These sounds would be familiar to them soon, the sounds of houses being placed on barges and towed out to sea. They would be painful, torturous sounds.

The final transport ship would be here soon: their last rites.

"I'm here to support what you're doing," Francis said, stumps buried deep in his jacket pockets, "but I won't put me saws in there. Me and the wife decided. They're all we've got, boys." As a young man, deep in the dark years of the depression, there had been a hollowness to his soul, an emptiness, contagious; the whole town, the province, was infected with it. His saws had filled that hole. He thanked the company for that, but he hated them now, more than he thought he could ever hate. And still, his wife, June, hated even more. *Goddamn that company. Goddamn them!* Spitting out the words, like poison. *That's our harbor out there, and they'll just walk away with her and leave us with nothing!*

A voice called over from the other side of the heap, "That's fine, Francis, boy."

Jack Trask, a camp bull, there next to him, patted his shoulder. "You're a good man. Damn good man. Don't worry."

A final splash of gasoline, a baptism, the flick of a lighter, and the pile ignited in a flash. Dirty black smoke, choking and toxic, billowed up. Flames licked the plastic, quickly melting it. Cracks and pops came out of it like fireworks.

Someone pointed and screamed at the conflagration, cursing the company, the bastards.

A horn blew, once, twice, a bellowing horn, a death call. Their death call. It was the last barge, early, down from Labrador, coming in from around the bluff. But the fog was too thick to see through, erasing everything.

Just past dawn, the sun was not fully risen.

The tools were a melted mess, charred and sludge-like, almost flat, indistinguishable from one another and no longer bubbling and coughing flames. There were just a few of the men left; the rest had gone, to continue drinking somewhere else, to forget. Empty beer boxes littered the ground like debris from an explosion. Francis was there, sitting, smoking. The fog was thinning, too, rolling out in thin wisps. The machines had stopped. It was quiet, and no one spoke as they listened to their own strangled breaths.

Francis stood, starting for the cove. "I'm heading down the way to see her off."

A few followed him. The rest stayed, staring at the last embers of flame.

At the bottom, out past the wharf, where it disappeared, they could see the outline of two ships poking out of the soupy grey: hull, bridge, the massive crane, but nothing else, just vague shapes: ghost ships. For years, this had been a hub of activity. Trucks would cart in timber from inland to be shipped upriver. Logs would carpet the river, men—chaulks for feet—dancing a strange dance, twisting and turning quickly, directed them with pike-arms. It was dead now and devoid of life—motors shut down, lights off, and the whole lot inoperative.

Standing on the beach, scanning the bay, the rocks slid and repositioned themselves beneath their feet. The wharf would be gone in a few hours, history, memory, quickly and efficiently dismantled and loaded onto the barge.

Flocks of sea birds were out, cawing, circling low, diving down. It was common enough to shoot them while jigging, to load up a .12-gauge and blast them right out of the sky. Francis saw himself doing this when he was young, gripping the barrel while he stood in his boat, an explosion of feathers spiraling down.

Paul Russell, on crutches, trying to steady himself, peered forward, listened to the fifteen- and twenty-footers knock off the wharf with the steady rhythm of the waves. It

73

was a familiar sound, like logs knocking off one another, like the tick of a clock. "She's quiet out there."

"Quiet, yeah," from behind him. Francis couldn't tell who; they all seemed to speak in the same dead, flat tone.

Francis went to the edge of the beach. There, moving in the tide, swaying with the driftwood and garbage, was a piece of cloth, dotted with patterns of tight circles of lavenders, reminding him of a lady's Sunday dress.

Still a little pissed, he wondered, *What is that there for?*

Instinctively, he bent and touched it. Reeled back. Fell against the rocks, face white and slack like dead skin. A grunt of pain: "Almighty Jesus."

Fingers—white, bloated, pecked at—clutched the cloth and poked out of the froth of the water. The tide drew back slowly and revealed an arm, a man's arm, skin ragged and hacked off where it had once met a shoulder, a cheap digital watch still around the wrist, ready to snap.

The wind blew, and, for a moment, the fog peeled back in places, revealing portions of the bay. The water was littered with limbs, dozens of them: arms, legs, hands, feet, bobbing like so many buoys, still wearing sleeves of shirts and legs of pants, rings, feet budging against laced shoes and green rubber boots, reminding them all of the cold deck. Patches of gulls floated amongst them, getting fat. He wished he had his rifle.

He'd seen corpses before, they all had: split, sawed, crushed. But not like this. No, not like this.

Francis stood up, put his mouth to his front pocket where he kept his cigarettes, like he'd done a thousand times, like he'd learned to do with no hands, like June had showed him. Shaking badly, unsteady: "Jesus, someone give me a light."

Jim Karate, eyes like dinner plates, head following the motion of the water: "Oh, dear God. They've had an accident. Francis, you've got the best legs. Get up over the hill, man. Get some help down here!"

Starting out to the wharf, Francis said, "Don't be foolish. Get out in the boats before the fog lifts. Forget the help. There's no need. We'll use the nets to haul them in."

"Think there might be someone alive in the water?"

The reality of it all had bit deep into him. "Christ, no one's alive in the water. They're all dead, sure. Don't be stupid; someone did them in. They've got themselves killed."

Stinking of saltwater and smoke, still tasting the water, Francis came home. June was at the stove, hovering over it, cooking. He was tired, more tired than he thought he could ever get, which reached deep into the fiber of his muscles and seemed to expand like a balloon. He sat at the table. "Get us a cup, will you, dear?" he asked her, thinking of the men casting sprawling nets and the continuous dead thud of limbs as they hauled in pieces of men, half-men, bits of men, torsos of men, while he worked the motor. The boat had quickly filled up, and they burned them on the beach, erasing and reducing it all to ash.

Before he went into the house, he had gone to the shed. His saws were there, hung up. He knew them like any other man knows his hands, each bump, blemish. He had touched them expecting to find them warm, out of gas, the blades worn just a little from cutting. But they were the same as he had left them, as he remembered them. She'd cleaned them well, June.

"Are they done?" she asked.

Someone did them in. "Done?"

"The company, boy."

"I don't know. Didn't bother to go down. No point, I suppose."

She brought him his cup. Her hair up in tight curlers, he saw her forehead was wind-burned, her lips and skin drawn. And there, in the creases of her knuckles, raw from scrubbing, like dark laugh lines, fault lines, were faint grease stains, oil stains, not unlike those that were now permanent stains on the skin of the men he had worked with, men with hands. He had never scrutinized any part of her before like he did now. Maybe, when they were young, when he lusted for her, he had, but now it was as if he were seeing her for the first time. Her fingers, though slender, had been worked hard, ground down and abused: nails chipped, knuckles callused. These hands had been worked—no resemblance to kitchen hands.

She brought the cup to his lips, and he took a sip, testing it. He thought of watching her sleep, of her sweating and turning. She was dreaming of her mother again, he knew. She was a good woman, the best. But he wondered, in all that goodness, if maybe those dreams had brought on a personal darkness. "Out in the garden this morning?" He could not hate her if she lied to him now.

"Garden...?" She held up her hands, her dirty hands. He looked at her face, her wide, intelligent face, her lovely face. Her eyes seemed to hang, tired, exhausted, and for a second he thought he saw fear and confusion take form. "Yes, I was out digging. I should've gotten to it before. But now is better than never. Besides, I didn't want you out there, the way you are lately."

Francis held her hand, kissed it. "Maid, you do too much already. Too much, my dear."

Stains of Life

I watch with growing anxiety as the hordes of elderly and mentally diseased begin to show up and mull around the transit station, waiting for the buses to arrive. It's a few minutes past nine; they are late.

These people remind me of stains on the sidewalk, dark leeches clinging to the brick walls. These are the dregs of the *new* society, the unwanted. I can't help but feel a deep disdain for them. I find their tattered and worn clothes disgusting. Constantly spitting, biting their nails with nervous anticipation, they pick through their lice-ridden hair and wait—all signs of addiction. Some mumble a crazed language only they are fluent in, some pray, others curse at the sky. Off to the side, a woman dances and hops around—schizophrenia, probably. Mental disease is common now that publicly funded treatment has ended and all the open hospitals are closed.

I'm sixty-five, recently retired. According to the government, I'm no longer of any use to them now, either.

I've feared this moment for years, decades. Everyone knows where the buses lead: the factories. They're not hidden from us. They're not a state secret. Several miles outside the city, you can see the smokestacks reach ominously into the sky like enormous brown pointing fingers. Dark clouds of thick black smoke bellow out, the sky dark with soot. They never stop.

At first, when the war had ended, mass shootings and electrocutions were used. This proved far too inefficient and costly. Gas was more effective, the Central Committee learned, and with the use of mass media, it became acceptable in the public mind. The unwanted are now marched in and out daily, like on a conveyor belt without end. They are sent there to suck in gas to keep them lulled, obedient. In *these* factories, nothing is made but death.

I will be sick with addiction soon, too. On my sixty-fifth birthday, only three days ago, I received notice that I was to appear at the 10th Terminal for transportation to Factory 12 at 9AM. I considered escape. *Run to the forests*, I told myself. But they would find me eventually, the man-made agents of the government, with their savage dogs and electric cattle prods. The homing device with which each and every one of us has been implanted has already determined that fact.

"Is this your first time?" a man asks, his voice rough and coarse, sandpaper.

I turn. He is elderly, my age, perhaps, but more used, ugly. His eyes are clear. He has not yet lost his mind to the smoke. Soon, though. I can tell. His skin is already grey and slack, his teeth yellow and his gums black. "Yes, my first," I reply. "Is it as bad as it seems?"

He scuffs his dirty shoes on the concrete and looks down. "I'm afraid so. But after the first few, you won't mind as much. It tastes like candy, the smoke. It's something they add to make the whole process easier—for them, not us."

He extends his hand. I shake it and introduce myself. "Adam. Adam Blanchard. I'm from Block 56. I used to be an engineer at the food processing plant."

"Cliff Henderson. Pleased to meet you. I was an environmental consultant. Not that it's any good to me now. At this point, all I'm good for is sitting at my terminal."

"Really, I can't understand this. It's hard to take in," I tell him. It's difficult for me to rationalize this process now, not like before, when I saw the whole of it as necessary. I'm not like most of the others. I'm educated, once very productive.

"I was like you, a few weeks ago. Now look at me. You see him?" He points to a young man squatting in a corner, picking through a pool of his own puke. "He was a physicist, an advisor to a minister. But he lost his mind."

Suddenly, there's a squelch of tires, a hiss of tires, and the crowd becomes frenzied. Already, they're beginning to line up by the curb, pushing and shoving anxiously, each one hoping to be the first on the bus, the first to get off and into the factory.

There are a dozen buses, maybe more, coming up the road in a line. They are clean and polished, sun reflecting off their aluminum exteriors. Advertisements are painted on the sides: smiling faces, happy people, youthful, having no resemblance to these poor wretches. The caption reads: *Be proud. Work hard.*

Cliff pats me on my shoulder. "Come on, we'd best hurry. I don't want to get fined."

"Fined?" I ask.

"Yeah, for a week. The last ten only receive a portion of their smoke. You get dreadfully sick. You want to die. But it keeps people obedient. I'm speaking from experience. You're exempt, since you're new. But you don't want to give the guards the wrong impression. They can be cruel."

The guards, synthetic and giant, muscles bulging beneath tight grey uniforms, far larger, far stronger, far more imposing than any man, form a kind of gauntlet, their faces hidden behind reflective visors, and herd the sick onto the bus like cattle. I hear whimpering, and I can smell singed cotton and skin, like plastic left on a heater. I hold my breath, waiting to be prodded as I step onto Bus 9, but nothing comes.

One guard scribbles on an electronic clipboard. I assume it's a head count.

My brain hurts. It's the first headache I've felt in almost ten years. My stomach wants to regurgitate the three breakfast supplements I took with calorie water an hour ago. I feel doomed. Sickness is something people like me have left behind in the past. The feeling is foreign, alien. I feel like my existence, my personal history, is being snuffed out, that I'm being raped. And as I step onto the bus, I realize I am now what the Central Government has defined as a "non-entity."

The low hum of the bus is hypnotic, and the seats inside are new and plush and comfortable, making me want to sleep. I voted for Bill-5968B, just like everyone else. Ninety-eight percent had been in favor of additional funding for the transportation of addicts to and from the factories. It was necessary, or so I had believed, to keep them passive, compliant.

"They don't want you thinking of where they're taking you. Later, when you've had a taste, you won't care so much," Cliff whispers. I guess he's been watching me doze off.

Through the outskirts of the city, the passenger's faces pressed against the windows, I watch with them as we pass the new housing units that have just gone up. Already, young, healthy families play outside, hair neat and trim, dressed in clean white uniforms. Their concerns are with the here and the now, just as mine had been, and not with the future, with the factories. Like them, I'd been unconcerned and ignorant, too.

Soon, it seems to turn to night. I look out the window. The smokestacks loom large. Smoke stretches across the sky like death, practically blotting out the sun. As the factories come into view, I'm surprised at just how small and insignificant they are—a few rows of small single-level buildings constructed of cinderblock with tar roofs. For miles around the factories, the grassy fields have all died, leaving a barren desert plain of dust and dirt.

The convoy of buses comes to a halt, and the passengers scramble to get off and in for their fix.

"Don't let appearances fool you. It isn't as innocent as it looks," Cliff says. "This is a terrible place."

I feel fixed to my seat, stapled there permanently. "I can't," I moan, my eyes fat and white with fear.

Cliff grabs me by the arm. "You'd better. There are penalties for those of us who are last off."

We file out and down a gravel path leading into the factory.

It is dark and quiet, and the air is stale. My first impression is of the back-alley surgery shops I've seen over the years, the ones with the greasy linoleum floors and water-damaged ceilings, kitchen sinks used to sterilize dirty scalpels and dinner tables used as gurneys. Hundreds of stations, reminding me of school desks, are lined in dozens of neat rows. People sit under small bright spotlights and wait. Hundreds of clear tubes run down from the ceiling, like snakes, to surgical masks on hooks. I hear a motor churning; I assume it's the smoke generator that's buried deep in the bowels of the factory.

"H-6489," a deep, emotionless voice says. I turn, and one of the guards is facing me, clipboard in hand, eyes hidden behind his reflective visor. "Come with me."

I follow him down an aisle of occupied stations. Towards the middle, the guard stops. "Sit here," he orders. "You are permitted fifteen minutes at the terminal. Then you must remove your mask and proceed to the front."

I sit down and immediately notice the digital clock— all zeros, dead eyes—and the red and green lights fixed to the front of the desk, just like my notice had explained. I had read the instructions over carefully a half dozen times, so I wouldn't forget. *When green light flashes, place mask over face. Timer will then begin—inhale deeply, exhale slowly. After fifteen minutes, the red light will blink twice. Remove mask and exit out of factory.*

I'm not sure whether or not I'll be able to go through with it. This *is* suicide, and I'll be dead in only a few short weeks.

Then the green light flashes, and I watch in horror as everyone around me places the masks on their faces in one simultaneous motion. They seem to breathe in unison, loud, deep, bassy.

Looking around, eyes darting fast, heart pounding, Cliff is nowhere to be seen. I'd hoped he'd find a seat next to mine, maybe help me through the whole thing. He seems like a friend, someone I can possibly trust.

One of the guards looks directly at me, waits for me to comply with procedure.

Nervous, sweating, I place the mask over my face. I can hear my quick breaths loud and deafening in my ears, hot beneath the plastic, stale, the rubber straps tight against the back of my head.

The clock starts up—tension rising in me—and a low whoosh comes from overhead. People start coughing; someone laughs. Then a soft hiss, and I can taste it, the smoke, like candy, just as Cliff said. At first, I try not to breathe. My eyes fill with water; tears streak down. I grip the chair, fingers digging hard into the plastic, thinking I can outlast the timer, my dosage. My head starts to feel light, as if it isn't attached to my body. Tiny sparks flash. Then calm overtakes me. I inhale, deeply this time, filling my lungs, not fighting it, and my head feels relaxed and separated from the rest of me. I remember being intoxicated once, as a young man, before alcohol was outlawed. It was not unlike that sensation, but without the nausea.

Through the haze, I see people go limp and drop over. They remain motionless, the masks still attached to their faces, fine streams of smoke coming out the sides.

Immediately, the guards are there with stretchers to pick them up and carry them away for disposal.

I should be shocked and abhorred by what I see. But I am not. I do not care. The smoke is pumping, numbing my central nervous system. The Central Committee's chemical engineers have done their jobs well. I feel good, unrebellious, satisfied. I'm sure that I am even smiling.

To the west of the city, we are unloaded into a large brick holding centre adjacent the bus terminal, which is not unlike a prison.

Pursuant to Law-8746J, addicts cannot occupy personal residences. Escapees, found squatting in the city, have become a persistent problem for the Central Committee. To eat, to survive, they sell smoke to the wealthy. There are always customers. This has resulted in large numbers of public executions, televised executions that are backed by massive advertising campaigns.

Inside, it's dark and cold. Only the deep red of the emergency lights is on, turning eyes, faces black. Everyone is a shadow. The narrow hallways are filled with heaps of dirt and pools of human waste. The smell is overpowering, and the flies are loud. Addicts clog the stairwells and couple everywhere in plain sight, like knots of surging flesh, paying no attention to who is watching. Others stand around coughing and spitting, clawing at their skin, already in need of another fix, holding onto the walls for dear life. I notice an old man slumped on the floor, his face and chest sunken in horribly, his jaw slack and yawning, his tongue fat and black, like a slug.

Cliff takes me to his room. It is small. A stained mattress is in one corner, brown stains, dried blood, I figure. There are no bathrooms or sinks, only a small meat bucket in the corner, already half-full.

The effects of the smoke seem to be wearing off already. I have a mild headache, a slight tremor in my hands, but I'm otherwise fine.

"When was the last time you saw the Cabinet on television?" Cliff starts, sitting on the mattress and looking worn down.

I shrug. I'd never cared much for politics; it's all a little too melodramatic for my tastes. Men in one-piece grey suits and jet-black hair, arms flailing. I still remember the immediate post-war years, when men like that were all too common. "I'm not sure. Two months, maybe."

"There's talk that some of them are addicted, too, or worse yet, dead. You can tell something is wrong. They haven't made any public appearances in weeks. Our trips to the factory are infrequent, and the smoke has been heavily rationed. Things have become disorganized. Not like before, when we'd be lucky to last a few days, when the smoke was thick and black and lethal. Disposing of us is low-priority now, I guess." He pauses, looks out into the hallway, up and down, nervous, and closes the door. "You seem like a reasonable man, unlike the rest of them. I feel I can trust you. Can I?"

"Sure. You can trust me."

A brief pause as he considers what he's about to say. "I've been planning my escape for several weeks now. I need your help."

"Don't be foolish, man. You know just as well as I do that there's no escape. What about your locator?"

He reaches down beneath the mattress and into a small slit that had been made along the side. His arm vanishes up inside. "I removed it," he says, matter-of-factly. I stare in horror as he holds out his hand and shows me a small silver microchip the size of a dime. He passes it to me and parts his hair, letting the dim light from the window fall on his pale white scalp, revealing a dark and ragged scar. "I cut it out with a piece of glass I smuggled in here when I first arrived."

Rolling the chip over between my index and forefinger, staring at it in amazement, seeing minute flecks of dried blood—*Cliff's* blood—in between the plastic and metal, I ask him, "Where will you go?"

A statement: "The forests."

I rub my forehead, feeling the microchip I too have hidden beneath my skin, embedded into my skull. "They'll find you. You *must* know that. They'll find you, and I'll see advertisements for your execution on the billboards as we drive out to the factories."

He goes to the window, calm and resolute. "I've thought about it. Even if I escape and end up starving in the forest, I don't care. I just don't want to die like the rest of these poor bastards. There's no dignity in it. Will you help me?"

For a second, I think about the woman who'd been waiting at the terminal, dancing, and the others at the factory, their skin like grey leather masks, their expressionless glassy eyes telling me that their minds are drowned, dropping over at their terminals. I can see them, the cords of their necks stuck out like piano wire, holding their masks tight to their faces and sucking the smoke, smiling. I'll be like that, soon enough. "Yes, I'll help you."

For days, Cliff speaks at length about his wish to see the forests before he dies, to escape into the wilderness and breathe one last breath of the fresh air, to have his lungs filled without the sickly sweet taste of smoke on his tongue.

Hidden in the sole of his boot, he has a tattered and badly worn photograph of a tree, neatly folded dozens of times. It was clipped from *National Geographic*, a magazine I haven't seen in decades. Most mornings, he sits at the edge of his mattress, runs his fingers over the outline of the branches and stares into it, like some religious ritual. He says he can still smell the leaves in autumn.

Myself, I no longer remember much of what lies beyond the city. Images of wildlife have long been labeled subversive, and the smoke has left my mind a vacuous space, the memories from my youth almost gone, erased, vanquished.

In the few brief weeks since my retirement, I've grown old. I feel weak, tired. Headaches pound my skull just hours after the smoke has made me giddy. In this place, this asylum of sorts, there are no mirrors. But I see my reflection in the windows. I look more and more like the others. My skin is slack and loose, hairless and dotted with dangerous-looking liver spots. It's obvious that I'm dying.

Cliff has not lost all hope, though. It keeps him alive, keeps the cancers at bay. I'm a pessimist; diseases billow up inside me, eat away at my organs. It's only a matter of days, not weeks or months.

But I've decided to take control of my destiny. I've decided not to die like the rest of the poor bastards out in the hallway.

We've been waiting for our moment—patient and always watching. But the guards are diligent, and time is of the essence.

If I can get to the edge of the forest, Cliff tells me, *I'm home free. The guards are afraid of the place, mortally terrified of it. They're programmed to fear it, just like everyone else. By the time they bring in search dogs, I'll be gone, though. But that doesn't matter. So long as I get to touch the trees, I'll die a happy man.*

I won't dare dream something so crazy. A carefully placed cattle prod to the back of my skull is about all I can hope for. Then I'll be rid of this place, this sickness that fills my lungs with fluid, and that's fine with me.

There were five deaths this morning. It's the most since I've arrived. From what I've heard, and Cliff seems to believe it, there was a mass suicide in the basement. *It's because they're rationing the smoke*, he tells me. This is true; we've both been sick, physically ill. There are whispers in the hallways that someone smuggled in a tin can, and the group used it to slit their wrists.

It's made the guards jumpy.

Cliff gave me his picture of the tree this morning, before the buses picked us up at the terminal. *Something to remember me by*, he said. *It'll keep your mind in a better place when you're going through the worst of it.*

Our plan is simple: I'm to go into spasms on the bus floor and fake a seizure, which is not uncommon. Once the two guards are distracted, Cliff will grab one of the cattle prods and make a run for the forest. Our only problem is getting him off the bus. If the driver won't open the door, even with a cattle prod stuck in his face, we're dead.

Frost has set in. A thin layer of sparkling white covers the shoulder of the highway, and the long grass is stiff and straight, unmoving. Winter is only a month away, at most. We know that even if Cliff escapes, even if he makes it to the forest, this is a suicide mission. He'll only last a few days. But we discussed this at length, and he doesn't care. *Anything is better than this*, he says.

I can see the smoke. Half an hour, and we'll reach the factory.

Withdrawal, I think, has really started to set in. The first signs of it came this morning. With each passing minute, it continues to well up in me. It makes my thoughts uneven and scattered; I can't concentrate on one thing for very long. I constantly want to vomit, but I hold it down. This new sickness has been coming on stronger each day for the last week, starting to torment me in the early morning, as if anticipating the arrival of the buses.

It's going to make things a little more difficult, but I'll get through it.

I'm on the outside seat. My hands are sweating. I rub them on my stained pants. This sweat is anxious sweat. I can see the factories, almost taste the smoke.

I don't have to convince myself that the guards will be fooled by my performance. I'm old, addicted, diseased; they have no reason to doubt me. There is a procedure they follow. They'll check my vital signs, carry me to the back of the bus and wait until we've arrived at the hospital, where they'll sit me at my terminal and place the mask over my face anyway.

I see the patch of broken pavement coming up ahead, the one I see every day. The bus will swerve to avoid the pothole. We do not wear seatbelts. I will be thrown from my seat. I've visualized this scene a hundred, a thousand times in my mind.

I close my eyes and wait. All I can hear is my heart beating loud and fast in my ears, slamming off my chest.

Cliff touches my hand lightly. It's his way of saying thank you.

The bus veers to the left. I fall onto the floor. I kick and thrash my legs around violently, spastically, my arms flailing, like I've been put in a vat of electrified water, doing some crazy dance on the floor. I start to spit and moan, rolling my eyes back in my head as far as I can get them to go.

"H-6489, please return to your seat." It is one of the guards. "H-6489," he repeats. "H-6489, return to your seat."

Some of the other addicts are getting excited, which we had hoped for. They'll keep the other guard busy.

I feel the heavy boots reverberate through the floor, the cool and lifeless hands on my throat, checking my pulse. He holds my arms tightly, his knee hard on my chest, like a thousand pounds. "Remain calm, H-6489," he repeats, like they'd all been programmed to do, as if I were somehow going to respond. "You will receive medical attention once we arrive at the factory."

Already, my body aches. I'm not sure how long I can keep up the charade. Cliff had better hurry and make his move, or he'll be staring at that picture for the rest of his short existence.

"Return to your seat, R-7560," the guard on top of me says.

There's a soft sizzling, and the smell of burnt rubber.

The pressure on my chest lets up some.

I open my eyes and see the guard fall over, his visor cracked, his face bleeding a light blue, like brake fluid.

I sit up, winded. I watch Cliff strike the other guard across the face in a long fluid swing with a cattle prod, leaving a horrible wide gash.

Its arms go wild, thrashing around, spinning, going haywire, knocking Cliff against the opposite row of seats, pirouetting, arms outstretched, looking like a crazy ballerina.

The guard falls to his knees and doesn't get up, clutching at his back, face contorting, lips split.

For a second, I see the driver's eyes in the rearview mirror, nervous eyes, darting from the road to the seats behind him, then to the road and back again, expecting the worst.

I have to act.

I run to the front of the bus. "Stop here," I tell the driver. He looks at me, not saying anything, continuing to drive. I put the cattle prod to his face. "Stop here." He refuses to comply.

Both hands gripping the handle tightly, knuckles white, I swing and strike him across the top of the skull. A large fleshy piece comes away, blue splashing the window in a kind of ugly Rorschach blotch. His head slumps forward and hits the horn. The bus swerves in a long and seemingly endless curve off the road, tires skidding.

Then it goes up on two wheels; the front dives down. I feel weightless. I can see the other passengers in mid-air, screaming hysterically, everything in slow motion, Cliff's face a grimace of pain and both the guards still, lifeless. We fall into the ditch and the bus tips to the left, the gravel coming towards us, fast. Then it hits, slams into the ground. Glass flies at my face, cuts, slices me in a hundred places.

For a moment, there is a kind of suspended animation, silence. No sounds. Nothing. I am dazed, barely conscious, a constant ringing in my ears, my body numb, in shock. Clouds of dust turn the inside dark, like night. Coughing, crying comes from the back.

In the next few seconds, things come to me like snapshots, sound bites. Pounding. Glass breaking. Grunting. Through the dust, someone wriggles out the side through a broken window, falls away from the bus and lurches forward, wounded, gripping his side. Gravel crunches.

Touching my face, fingers coming away bloody, feeling weak, confused, I kick at what's left of the door and crawl out, too.

I stare at the staggering figure. R-7560. No, *Cliff*. I feel my mind clear just a little; my head lifts some. *Cliff's headed toward the forest. Yes, that's it. That's what we'd planned.*

Hauling myself up, hurting, the others screaming from inside, wailing, I call out. Cliff turns and motions for me to follow. Stepping forward, I collapse. My knees give way beneath me. He keeps going, tells me to hurry, there's no time.

I look up and see the clouds, see the bleak horizon again, somehow darker than before.

Weak, blood leaking out my face, pouring down across my chest in rivers, addiction swells up in me now, bubbles over.

It's been a day or more since I've been to the factory, and my body can still remember the numbing sensation of the chemicals coursing through my veins, washing away pain and bad memories. Somewhere distant in my mind, a familiar voice calls out, tells me to stay and sit and wait. *Everything will be fine. The smoke heals.* It's a comforting thought, warm, inviting.

Out on the field, I can see a dot of a man, running, turning, screaming to me, crying my name, wanting me to follow him, begging.

My body decides against it. "I can't. There's no point. I have to wait for the next bus. They'll be here soon. I don't want to miss it!" I call out. "I haven't been to the factory today."

Beneath Ground

"There they go again," Marty said, sitting up in bed, grinding his fists into the comforter, gritting his teeth.

Jen was annoyed, more with her husband than with the thumps and knocks and moans. Hot-tempered and belligerent, he was his father's son; she'd known it for years, maybe longer. "Can't you just let it go? They're not all that loud, anyway." Maybe they were, but certainly no louder than the twenty-somethings they'd been sandwiched between at their last wasteland of an apartment. She tugged at his arm. "Just go back to sleep."

Too late. He was already up, dressed, storming into the kitchen. "They said we'd have quiet. They said we wouldn't even know they were up there. Well, by Christ, if they don't quit that racket, we'll be out of here pretty goddamned quick. And they can forget about that lease agreement." Jen could see his back bent, ass sticking out of the porch closet. His voice, muffled: "They're sixty-fucking-five! What could they possibly be doing this time of night? It isn't fucking, I assure you. You've seen her—she's no prize."

Sitting up, still half-asleep, staring at the alarm clock, numbers fuzzy double-zeros: "Tomorrow, I'll ask them to keep it down, that's all. Just stop. Come to bed."

Marty emerged, broom in hand, brandishing it like a weapon. "Hell with that. We can't let people walk all over us, Jen." He knocked the end of the broom on the ceiling. "Shut up! *Shut it!*"

Jen huffed in frustration. "You know—"

Suddenly, the racket ceased.

"See, what did I tell you?"

She threw the covers up over her. "Yeah, you deserve a medal, hero." It was her usual response to his stupidity. Always gut-shot him. Since they'd lost the baby, hurting was about the only thing left they had in common.

"Why do you talk shit like that? Not like I'm the one starting all the goings-on. I'm not the one—"

More noise came down on them: scratching, long and drawn out, cat's claws running along carpet, and then a deep bassy hum, a crazy and disorganized baritone choir. Glass smashed, then more knocking and scratching.

They waited, listened.

"What—"

"Shush!" Marty said.

For a few moments, there was nothing. Silence. Outside, a car sped by, tires screeching, headlights blaring through the blinds, creating a ghostlike searchlight glow. Then, more scratching.

Jen got up with Marty, listened intently, looked up, the blanket tight around her shoulders.

"I'm calling up there."

"Wait," Jen said. "Hear that?"

Putting his ear to the wall: "I hear talking, I think. They're talking. I can almost make out what they're saying."

This was not unlike the game they played from time to time, ears pressed tight against the wall, trying to find the best position, trying not to breathe, television muted as they listened in on the quarrels and spats of their neighbors. The real juicy stuff kept them amused, kept them distracted from hating each other. Strange now, though. The couple upstairs was elderly, in the twilight of their years, their petty arguments part of ancient history.

"Someone's moaning."

"Moaning?"

"Listen."

Jen put her ear to the wall. She could hear it, coming down through the beams, reminding her of a didgeridoo. Stepping back: "What's going on up there?"

Face tight, jaw clenched, she saw he was losing his patience. Eyes closed, forefinger and thumb bracing his temples, breathing hard between his teeth, emphasizing each syllable: "That's enough. I'm going up there—"

Something crashed, like a chair exploding against a wall. It was louder than anything before, almost on top of them, in the room with them.

Jen gasped and grabbed for Marty.

"*Enough already!*" The words barely out, Marty swung a quick jab at the wall, leaving a dirty ragged little hole of broken plaster and chipped paint.

"Now look what you've done," Jen said, forgetting the noise. "Had to, right? Who's going to fix that?"

"It's nothing." He was already inspecting the damage. "I'll fix the hole later. It's not a big deal."

"Hear that? They've stopped again."

Silence. The only sound the smooth hum of the bedroom fan.

"Jen..." Marty said, picking at the fist-sized indentation. "Jen, you got to see this. Jen?"

"What?"

"Look in the hole. I'll get a flashlight and hammer."

Nervous: "What? Are there rats? Tell me there's no rats, Marty."

"No rats. Just look."

Jen pressed her face close, expecting to find dust and termites, the back of the opposite wall, but past the exposed wooden frame, the electrical wiring and copper pipes, all she saw was black. A waft of cold air billowed up and stroked her cheek, bringing with it the smell of rot. For a second, she thought she saw a light flicker, candlelight, perhaps, a dot of a flame, insignificant. No, *impossible*.

Marty was back, moving her.

Confused, she grabbed him by the arm. "You see that? Do you see that? There's something *in there*."

Anxious, Marty tore at the wall with the beveled end of the hammer. Jip-rock came loose in strips; pieces fell to the floor. Dust in the air, flashlight turned on and held between Marty's teeth, Jen watched, hugging herself, the hole quickly becoming a ragged little doorway almost reaching to the floor and big enough to climb through.

A full draft came up at them, choking them, smelling bad, reminding her of fruit cellars.

Marty stopped, wiped sweat from his face, leaving a white streak of gypsum. He turned on the bedroom light. Coughing, holding his hand over his mouth in disgust: "What in Christ is the stink?"

Jen cried, "I... I don't know. I don't know, Marty."

They could see into the hole now, down into the darkness. The flashlight revealed a cavern, traced sharp rocky edges of the walls, as if it were some massive and ugly gullet. Neat steps winded slowly, turned right and opened up twenty feet down. The light flickered again, the candlelight moved, danced along the walls. Someone was down there. They could hear feet scuffing, dragging.

Marty called out, "Who the fuck is down there, huh? I'm armed!"

The light went out.

He turned to Jen. "Stay here," he said, climbing into the hole.

The flashlight bobbed, and Jen watched him descend. She could see the walls, grey and dry, as if they'd been there for years. Petrified roots stuck out like broken, arthritic fingers.

"I can't see anything yet." He reached the bottom and turned right. "Holy Jesus, Jen!"

"What?"

"You've got to take a look at this."

"What do you see?"

"There's everything down here. Must be a storage area of some kind. Get the landlord. There's no way he knows about this. He would've told us if he did."

"But what do you see?

"The place is chalked full of old junk. You've got to see this, Jen. Just go get the landlord first."

For a moment, there was nothing. Then: "Who the *fuck* are you, buddy? How did you get down here?"

"Marty?"

His voice went nervous: "Don't come any closer. I mean it!"

"Marty, I'm scared. Who else is down there? What's going on?"

The bottom of the tunnel flooded with light as Marty slowly backed out into it, hammer raised, a weapon. For a second, he turned, looked up toward her, mouth open like a gasping fish, about to say something, fear pasted all over him, making her gut send shockwaves up through her. Someone reached out from the shadows, hands white like alabaster, grabbed him by the legs and jerked them out from under him. The hammer flew, somersaulted in the air, and Marty was thrown onto his back. He flipped onto his belly, grabbed, clawed at the ground, but was hauled off into the room and out of sight.

"Help me! *Help!*"

"*Marty?*" Jen cried, clutching her face.

Screams, loud and harsh, echoed up. Marty's screams. Furniture crashed. Other voices, guttural. Not voices—a diseased dog's growl. Then another cry, piercing. Marty's cry was cut off.

Silence.

The flashlight fell to the ground, lay there like a dead animal, casting two ugly long shadows on the wall, which danced, flailed, merged and bore down. Then there was the sound of clothes ripping, tearing.

Jen was unable to move. She was fixed to the ground; her mind was frozen. In her mind, she saw his face and only his face. Tongue dead meat in her mouth, his name the only word she could form: "...Marty?"

More growling, savage and animalistic, came up and sounded hungry and desperate. She was sure there was at least a pack of them.

Marty is gone, she told herself. She knew it.

Then something in her snapped, broke like a severed artery, drowning out the real, and the animal in her took over. She ran out of the apartment, around the side of the house, the image of Marty lying at the bottom of the tunnel caught, paused, freeze-framed in her mind. She went up the front steps, pounding her fists on the door. Screaming, crazed screams, she begged for help, screamed to be let in.

The lights flicked on. Footsteps came down towards the door, and someone told her to wait, they're coming.

The door opened, and she collapsed inward.

"Oh, Jesus. What's wrong, Jen? What's wrong?" The voice was a man's voice, older and warm. "Where's Marty? Is there something wrong with Marty?"

She pulled at his housecoat desperately, tears and snot streaking down. "They killed him. They killed him. I know they killed him."

Bringing her inside, he closed the door. "What's going on? Did you and Marty have a fight? We thought we heard some goings on down there."

"No. No. *No!*" The last word was a shriek. Shaking her head, hauling at her hair, face buried in his chest, she was hysterical. "They took him. They took him. Behind the wall. *They were behind the wall!*"

The old man sat her down on the staircase, and knelt by her, hands on her knees, looking up. "I'll get my gun, and we'll look. Does that sound fine?"

She nodded.

"Just stay calm. We'll straighten things out. I promise," he told her and went back down the hallway.

A weight bore down on her, pushed her head between her legs, which felt like a sickness had invaded her. Let *him* go down the hole. Not her; no, never her. Not to see Marty like an ugly wreck on the highway, spilt across the tarmac; nothing left but bits of greasy meat.

A door closed behind her, and soft footsteps came down the hall. There was the hard snap of a breech rifle loading. "The wife and I agreed that it was best to get things out of the way now, rather than later."

Jen turned and saw a dark, solid shape coming straight at her as the landlord, a few steps up, brought the butt of the rifle down on her face quick and hard.

There was instant hot white pain. She fell over, slumped against the door, her ears buzzing, face numb. She could taste warm blood on her lips, her throat filling up with it, too. Barely able to breathe, almost choking, she saw the shoe rack at a horizontal angle.

Someone was talking. The voice sounded deep and dragged out, like slow motion. "I hope you're right about Marty. Saves me the trouble of feeding them. I can't keep this up much longer, anyway. I'm too old."

Grabbing her arm and lifting her up, he braced her weight against him.

Black swallowed her whole.

She was dreaming of the baby again, of finding her still and unmoving and quiet, smiling and peaceful, eyes closed, as if sleeping. She thought she was between breaths. Seconds stretched on endlessly. She said her name, touched her face. But her skin was cold, unnaturally cold. Then she noticed the thin trail of white coming from the corner of her mouth, which was hidden beneath the pillow.

"Wake up, bitch!"

No, not in the baby's room. The world was black, and she was tied down tight. Tired and nauseous and wanting to vomit, her mouth was full, stuffed with cotton socks; she could taste the bleach.

The voice was a man's voice, deep. "Get up, I said." Instant sharp pain spread out across her check in hot webs and connected with the low dull throb emanating from her nose.

She pried her eyes open.

She was beneath ground, where Marty went, but there was no Marty. The walls and floor were earth, and the place was lit with candles. The room was small, dark and wet. The floor and walls were earth. Like an old woman's house, it was crammed with useless junk: broken dinner chairs, dented paint cans, piles of knotted extension cords, rusted trunks, bicycle wheels, stained stuffed animals, rotten and tilting dressers, a rusted-out bassoon. Pictures were hung like wallpaper: velvet black panthers, paint-by-numbers, cheap reproductions of sailboats. A dirty cheap rug had been laid down beneath her feet.

A hole, a rat's hole, but much bigger, was carved into the wall to her right.

"Wake up, I said," the voice demanded.

She turned. The landlord, standing to her left, stared at her with his arms folded. "Dug out this place, oh, just when me and the wife first got married. Going to be an A-bomb shelter; couldn't afford to finish her, though. Doesn't matter anymore."

Ghost whispers came out from the hole, like soft wind through fall leaves, and something shifted in the dirt.

Checking his watch: "They're early. Figured they'd be a little late, seeing how they already ate this evening."

She started crying, muffled with her mouth full and taped tight, and knowing that Marty, *her* Marty, had been the meal.

"They're never happy, you know. No matter what I bring down, they always want more. Look at all this crap, sure."

Lighting a cigarette and moving to the dresser, chipped and painted yellow, he opened the top drawer. She saw an assortment of old and rusted tools inside. He selected a small saw: ugly, teeth missing, a hammer, the grey wooden handle cracked and held together with black electric tape, and two rusted garden trowels.

She tried to scream. Thrashing, the legs of the chair tipped and danced on the dirty rug as she watched him lay the tools out in a neat line at the edge of the hole like surgical instruments.

Smoke coming out of his nostrils in thick streams: "They like to divide the meat up equally. Everyone gets a fair share down here."

Eyes moved, shifted in the dark hole, a dozen red hungry eyes, blood eyes, tumbling over one another. Hands, grey and dirty, snatched the tools.

"Best get going. They're not too picky when it comes to meat," he said. Turning, he left, anxious.

There was the heavy panting and the click, click, click of the tools coming together, as if being sharpened. She thought of massive forks and knives and butcher shops and fatty beef hanging from glinting hooks. She felt her pants get wet, knowing she'd pissed herself, and waited for ugly white faces to come out and form in the dim light, to cut her up, to *trim her of meat.*

Long and painful minutes passed. They sat and waited and stared out at her.

"Those things he told you weren't true. You're different; not like the rest. But he doesn't need to know that."

One of them crawled out on all fours. Eyes sunken in, hair long and matted and caked in filth, it was dressed in a dirty three-piece suit that was much too small, the cuffs starting a few inches below the elbows. She saw that it had no shoes, and that its nails were long and black and talon-like. It smiled, and between its black worm-lips were teeth filed and sharpened down into needles.

It stood up and walked to her, a shaky walk. A grimace of pain stretched across its face. "You'll help us, won't you?"

Jen pushed herself back in the seat with her heels as far as she could, pulling at the restraints.

It brushed the hair from her face lightly, carefully. "We won't hurt you. Your man was another story. We'd listen to him most nights and wonder how you put up with him. All we want is to go back up top. You'll help us, Jen? Jen, right, isn't it?"

A system of intricate tunnels—tight and cramped, held up with dresser drawers, table legs and hockey sticks, pools of condensation dotting the floors like a turn-of-the-century coalmine—had been dug beneath the streets, the dirt deposited in a huge pile on the outskirts of the subdivision.

Winter was a dreaded thing. Fast approaching, the half-built houses they spent nights in—skeletons of houses, just foundations and frames, tarpaulins flapping in the wind like ragged bed sheets—had been rushed before the first snow hit, forcing them back under to the collapsed passageways that had drowned dozens in dirt, the starvation and disease that had eaten away at a good number of them.

To survive, to live, going back up had become a necessity.

There were no women left, either. Pregnancy had become a curse, swelling bellies like cysts and spewing forth stillborn, half-made children, killing all the mothers. Some of the babies were preserved in mayonnaise jars on a dirt altar. A small mound of gifts—broken bottles, soiled diapers, tattered stuffed toys—had been made as an offering of forgiveness. Jen saw them on their knees crying, wailing in grief, and she remembered clawing at the tiny casket as they lowered her baby down, the wrenching sadness eating at her like a cancer, drowning her mind. Covered in mud and dirt, refusing to believe, slamming her fists against the aluminum, dashing the flowers away, begging them not to bury her baby.

"What'll happen to them—the families—when you go back up top?" Jen asked.

A scar running deep just beneath his chin—*a suicide scar?*—his voice sounded choked, constricted, weak: "We have to eat."

She thought of Marty and of what she found that was left of him. At the end of one of the new and incomplete cul-de-sacs, an oven and chopping block fashioned out of an old oil stove, the fire already stocked, smoke rising up through the manhole, legs without feet, skinned, not looking like legs anymore, just meat and bone, ready to be cooked. Hysterical, he'd come to calm her, hold her. "He shook her. He shook her until she stopped. We could hear it down here. We listened. He stole her from you. You know that, right? He deserved this."

She nodded, heavy sobs coming from deep within her.

Smiling: "Don't worry about that now. You're home."

"Home?" she asked.

His head low, he took her hand in both of his. She could tell that he had been handsome once, traces of it still there, hiding somewhere in his deformed features. There was shame and sadness in his eyes, too, she recognized like an old friend.

"You stayed. A lot come down, but only a few stay. Even after you found Marty, you stayed. You're one of us, Jen."

For a week, she waited with them in the cold and damp of the underworld, watching as they got ready to go back up top.

Garden tools were turned into vicious and lethal looking things: rusty nails driven through table legs, spades on chains, broken gravel rakes taped lengthways to flagpoles, barbed-wire gloves.

A map, improvised in the dirt of the floor, outlined the attack route.

It'll be a slaughterhouse, Jen thought, seeing blood-soaked couches, *The Simpsons* dull and murky behind television screens splashed with red, like drowned faces beneath shallow water.

Fresh food, almost non-existent, was finally brought down on the eighth day. A frenzied crowd, a wild and starved crowd, was waiting, expectant, and reached desperately for a small morsel. It was fresh, uncooked, *raw*.

"Hurry," Worm Lips said, waiting back with her. "You'll have to be quick if you want eats."

Pushing through, from curiosity, not hunger—no, she'd *never* eat what they ate—she saw their dinner: *dog meat*. Large—a German shepherd, maybe—it was a household pet: fur clean and trimmed neat, teeth and nails polished. The animal was on its side, eyes dead and tongue lying flat on the ground, stomach yawning, ribs poking out like fangs, its limbs wrenched off like turkey legs.

One of them had its collar around its neck, mouth ringed in blood, laughing, grunting, getting down on all fours, imitating a dog.

The rest were entertained.

"We eat what we can get," Worm Lips told her. "It's rare for us to have meat like this, and we need our strength."

Jen felt hot bile rise in her throat. She'd seen them eat rats, beetles—one swallowed down another's steaming shit—but nothing like this.

She moved back, pushed against the dirt wall, away from the crowd and the hot copper smell that filled the room. "I can't."

Worm Lips, concerned: "Not hungry?"

"I... I can't."

"But you must. We're going up tonight. For me then?"

"...Can't."

Taking her hand, caressing it like a lover: "Soon then, maybe."

There was a war out on the streets. It was Sarajevo, or Beirut, maybe.

A police siren squawked. A man's voice, bellowing through a bullhorn, issued orders, demands. Then a series of sharp cracks were fired off.

From where she was lying, tied down, kitchen table hard against her back, she heard windows crash, front doors splinter, the screams of her neighbors.

The phone rang several times, like an alarm, an early distant warning system. She wondered if there were messages, a pleasant pre-recorded voice, a beep, pleading screams, a dial tone cutting them off abruptly.

It was quiet now. A calm, thick and unnerving, blanketed the neighborhood. Sharp shrills still rang out intermittently, children's cries, children who had hid in the back of closets and in laundry baskets and had been discovered.

During all of this, they came in from the streets, one after another, mounting their bodies on her, pressing their bony ribs against her breasts, planting their seed in her, stinking hot meaty breath on her face.

There were only brief pauses in between, like now. And her groin was no longer raw and burning, just numb.

Blindfolded, like she asked, the world was black, but she wanted this—at least, she wanted what came of it—but she couldn't have their eyes, wide lust eyes staring down at her, only inches away, watching them watch her, tongues tracing over broken picket fence teeth.

The front door opened, and she felt the cold between her legs, the wet sending shivers up through her.

"I'm going to untie you now, Jen," Worm Lips said.

He hadn't been in her. He'd been there the whole time, giving instructions, directions, holding her hand, keeping the rest of them to their business.

Voice calm, reassuring, comforting: "You can get down."

Taking the blindfold from across her face, he left so she could dress; her clothes were laid in a neat pile, folded beside the table, new and fresh and clean, stolen from a raided house.

Flashes of white raced past the window, ghosts. Sharpened garden tools, held high, glinted under the patio lights. Then there were screams, shrieking, as another one of her neighbors was snuffed out in the trees behind the house.

The back door opened and closed.

Jen turned.

A man was backed up tight to the door, covered in dirty splashes of thick red, his face masked with it. His eyes were wide and crazy, and there was too much white showing. His chest rose and fell, heaving. He was being hunted, and reminded her of a wounded deer, weak and pathetic looking, tired and confused.

He rushed her, grabbed her by the shoulders. Up close, she saw the balding crown of his head for the first time, the dark grey sacks beneath his eyes. It was the old man, the landlord. "Help me! You have to help me. They're everywhere, killing everyone. Do you have a gun, *anything?*"

"Let go," she demanded.

Squeezing her, out of his mind: "*A gun?*"

He would kill her for a way out. She could smell the desperation off him like cheap cologne. "Let go, I said."

He reached back and slapped her across the face, sending her sprawling across the kitchen floor. "Is there a gun, weapons, anything? *Answer me!*"

She said nothing, just stared up at him.

He went to the cupboards, rifling through them, searching, sending teacups and plates spilling out and crashing.

Jen reached behind her, to the china cabinet, to one of the drawers. She found plastic, cold steel. The knife was long and dangerous, something to keep away from children, to carve turkeys with.

Holding it for a moment, gripping it tight, feeling it, knowing the damage it could do, she sprang and jammed it into his right knee, twisting it hard until it found a home. Blood pumped out in thick streams, running down the hilt and across her arm, and she saw the triangular tip poking out the other side.

He buckled, fell to the floor and hauled at the knife. Screaming, unable to free it: *"Fucking bitch!"*

Compelled, some inner voice demanding from her, she selected a corkscrew and meat cleaver, and started slicing and stabbing him, crazed. Arms up to protect himself, bits of meat and bone flew back until she got at his face, quickly silencing him.

Worm Lips ran to her from outside. "Are you alright? We've been hunting him through the streets for hours. Got his wife. She was easy, asleep. He's crafty, though."

A dark red pool inched out from the back of her landlord's head. She knelt, dipped her finger in it, leaving a greasy streak in the linoleum. It tasted hot and warm, salty.

"I'll be fine," she said, taking him by the belt, the easy way, the way they showed her. He was old, frail, thin, and not heavy. Starting for the bathroom, to hang and bleed him out in the bathtub until morning, she reassured him: "We'll be fine."

Open 24/7

"N ow, you're sure that you won't mind working overnights?" the manager asked. She looked young, thirty-something. It would be easy to get away with a lot with her, rather than some old bitch that had been doing the same monotonous routine and had seen dozens of other guys like Tony come and go: professional slacker, expert loafer.

"Nope. Not at all."

"Sure?"

Tony nodded. "Sure."

"Okay. Well, I'd best show you what needs to be done around here when you're on. You'll do a few shifts with Adam first, then the store's yours. As you can see, the place is small. Really, overnights are for cleaning and restocking the shelves. At most, you might get half a dozen customers, so there'll be hours of nothing but silence. Like to read?"

"Voraciously."

"Then this job is something you might enjoy. First, though, I made a list. Just general stuff: sweep, mop, dust. The cigarettes have to be counted, and so do the scratch tickets, for insurance purposes, in case we get robbed. Oh, and don't forget to lock the door after twelve. You buzz people in after that, but don't let anyone in that looks scruffy. You know what I mean? We were held up here a few weeks back. Did you see the piece on the news?"

He had. "Sure. Did he take much?"

"Not really," she said, huffing. "A dozen cartons of cigarettes, some Nevada tickets. We keep the cash low— you do a drop for every hundred—so he only got eighty dollars and change. And before I forget, don't sell beer after two."

"You won't have to worry about that with me. I worked security for a few years. Harassing drunks don't scare me none."

"Great. The last thing I should mention, and this is probably the most important piece of advice you'll hear from me, or from anyone who's worked the overnights, is to invest in a thick blanket."

"For...?"

"Your window." She made a motion with her hands like she was hanging laundry on the line. "The first week or two will be killer. Not easy to get to sleep when you know the sun is shining outside. You might go two days without sleeping. It can be hard. I'm speaking from experience. But some guys who've worked for me never had a problem with it. I hope you're one of those."

"Yeah—me, too. I need at least seven hours, or my brain feels like it's made of lead."

Burning. Scorching. The red eye of the sun blared down, searing his brain. It was like an h-bomb had gone off outside. The blanket, one of those thick feather-down jobs from Sears, was x-rayed, a dull light passing through. Choking heat had filled the room, smelling of stale scotch and sour cheese, making it hard to breathe. The fan was on, blowing it back in his face, on to drown out the kids squawking and bawling on the street.

And his head—

(*Oh, dear Christ, my head!*)

—splitting down the middle, like it'd been cleaved in half with a hatchet. Painkillers and flu medication had made him worse off. He felt doped, groggy, uneven—yet still unable to sleep.

The mattress had become his nemesis, shifting beneath him. Lumpy and old, its coils bit into his side. It disdained him, Tony was sure, taking revenge for years of abuse. Tormenting him, it whispered its secret language of squeaks. He would shake the railing, punch it, curse it, twist it, command it to stop. For a brief moment of lucidity, he would calm down, get beneath the covers, breathe, try to get his heart rate down again. His eyes would get heavy. *So this is what it's like to fall asleep. I'd almost forgotten. I'm losing it. I've got to get a hold of things. Calm down... It's been five days. Yes, you'll sleep. Let it take you.*

Then the bed would laugh, and the sun would burn brighter. He would pop more pills—

(*I'll only take two more, no, four, just to be sure about it.*)

—and lie in wait for the inevitable.

For the last few days, he had lived in two worlds, walked a thin line: the dream state and reality. He wished they'd merge and get it over with.

"Ten eighty," Tony said, his voice sounding monotone, lifeless. He hated late night customers, the fat smelly ones, the kind with faded black jogging pants and greasy sweatshirts. It was like they were pre-programmed to be smug and arrogant. They made him uneasy, too. This one had been in every night this week, trying to make small talk. He had real bad psoriasis, and the cracks of his hands were stained in oil and grease. He looked inhuman, like a troglodyte being from beneath the Earth: skin white and waxy, having never seen the light of day, a drop of Vitamin-D.

Standing on the other side of the counter, he seemed to move in a kind of wave, left to right, right to left, his eyes staring. Tony was sure he could see through him—no, *into* him—right into the centre of his brain, right into his cerebral cortex.

Periodically, Tony looked down at the butcher knife kept under the counter. He could see it stuck in this guy's head, blood spurting out in thick glistening jets, pumping across the Nevada ticket case. He could feel his hand inch towards it, readying himself, just in case the small talk turned crazy.

"You sure it's that much, buddy?" he asked, his voice hoarse. He was a smoker and reeked of stale tobacco. It was poison, the smell. Tony could feel it burn the inside of his nose, singe the hairs there. "Down the road, they only charge me nine fifty."

"Then go down the road," Tony said, trying to sound firm, but his words came out sluggish.

The man rubbed his greasy beard and huffed. "Nah, I'll keep them." He motioned to open the door and turned. "Say, you hear them back there tonight?"

Tony looked at him, puzzled. "What?" He hated when they tried to make conversation.

"Don't play dumb. You know who. You hear them in the back from time to time."

"What are you talking about, buddy?" Nervous, Tony's fingers were on the handle of the blade, ready to make a swipe, cut the guy's nose off, make him an amputee. Adam said not to take chances. *Ever.* Addiction to painkillers— the crazy stuff, the stuff that doctors used to dull the pain cancer patients suffered, the stuff that made you wild and got you sick—had become a problem around town. Kids were out of their mind, robbing corner stores and cabbies to pay for them. The blade usually scared them off before you had to do something drastic.

"You'll see. They'll show you. I don't think you're ready for them yet. Soon." The guy's mouth seemed to move out-of-sync with the words, just a little, a fraction of a second behind, like in some bad Italian horror movie. He unwrapped the pack of cigarettes, put one in his mouth and pocketed the rest. "Once you *do* see, it'll be great, the sleep: unbelievable. For a few, it can be disastrous. But *they'll* decide that, not you."

Then he walked out, the electronic bell ringing over the door.

Tony sighed and rubbed his eyes, taking his fingers off the black plastic handle, trying to shrug off sleep, telling himself that he wasn't going to let *that* fuck in again. Another crazy had been in the night before, smelling of piss, flecks of dried vomit stuck in his beard, crying, looking for his cats. At least the druggies were obvious; they had an agenda. Who knew what these ones were capable of?

He started in on the mopping. It was just past three— no more customers until about five, at the earliest.

Scraping gum off the floor, his eyes felt flooded. His mind wandered, dreaming. For a second, as brief an image as an image between channels on television, he saw in his mind a dark lake—a black puddle, overexposed, an extreme close-up—and staring red eyes, burning eyes, eyes of fire flying past like a phantom.

He was starting to see things out of the corners of his eyes: human shapes, moving. Then he would look, and they were gone, jumping out of sight. Adam had warned him about it. This was more of that, he figured. Not real, just part of sleep deprivation, like that tank in *Altered States* where Jeff Bridges saw God and the beginning of all creation flash before him in the darkness.

Drawing in a deep breath, he pried his eyelids apart and hoped sleep would come later like a deluge, but he knew it was unlikely.

Tony had slept for three hours that day. It was a record, a *miracle*. That made twelve hours in eight days. His wife said that he was starting to look old, haggard. *Think it's best that you keep the new job? Maybe you should look for something else.*

113

Lately, Tony was forgetting things: where he put his wallet, phone numbers, the woman who seemed to occupy the house with him, her name. *Joanne...? Janet...? Something.* She was loud, too, and her voice echoed in his skull. During the days, he could hear her out in the living room, talking on the phone, laughing. Was she talking about him? Probably. No, he was sure of it. Conspiring against him. Yes, that was it! She wanted him gone, away from her. He would push a pillow over his head, hoping to drown her out. She was still there, though, her feet pounding down on the floor as she stomped to the kitchen and then back to the sofa again.

Once, he had felt sleep come over him—his eyes heavy, his thoughts random and incoherent, his mind showing images, warming up for the real show. Then she would come in looking for clothes in the closet. *Are you asleep? Sorry, just need a pair of jeans.* His heart would accelerate; his blood would run fast. He would think of killing her, smashing her, dropping her from their second floor apartment, head first.

This was all part of her plan, her vicious scheme to eradicate him, erase his mind, replace him with a mindless and false Tony.

She was probably waiting, waiting until he was at his weakest. Then she would strike with the deathblow. She was cruel, and who knew what she was capable of?

Something had to be done—sooner, rather than later.

Even here, at the store, sleep was impossible. He had picked the lock on the manager's office—she had an old ratty sofa—and three times he went in to lie down, all unsuccessful. If only he could get a few hours—

(*Forget the buzzer, forget the complaints, just sleep, man, sleep!*)

—he could figure Janet out, learn what she was really up to.

But the white noise of the place kept him up, the low buzzing constant, unending: refrigerators, halogen lights, computers, ice cream coolers. *Tumors! They can cause tumors to breed in your brain. I saw it on television once.*

He was sure they were speaking to him in their electronic language, like the bed: *Sleep? No one sleeps here. It is an endless night here, buddy.*

Then there was the beer cooler. Someone was back there tormenting him, opening and shutting the door when he wasn't looking. He could hear the footsteps, scuffing on the dusty tiles, their whispers. He had gone back dozens of times, moving cases, tearing the place apart, searching.

They were back there, somewhere. Hadn't someone told him they were there? A customer? Someone...

He was drinking coffee like water, trying to stay alert, keep his central nervous system on DEFCON-4. Eventually, they would show themselves, and he had to be ready. He would have them then. This was *his* store; they were the intruders.

She was crying, clutching at her hair. Her voice had taken on a high-pitched shrill—one octave higher, and only a dog would be able to hear it. "You're falling over the edge, Tony! Just quit the fucking job! Don't be stupid. This isn't worth it. *You're a god-damned wreck!*"

She was playing games again, playing them *her* way, telling him one thing and meaning something else, confusing him, warping his mind even more. Tony knew everything she said was shit. It was in her eyes: they had gone black, black as oil black. She might as well just come out with the truth and drop the charade, drop all the pretenses. She was an imposter.

She had found his stash and had confronted him. He had been keeping food under the bed, away from her. Who knew what she had been putting in it? Rat poison? Something worse? *She's out of options. Her only way to stay hidden is to claim utter and total ignorance.*

"*Liar!* You tell them it'll end soon. I'm on to them. You'll see."

She pleaded, the tears rolling. "Who, Tony? *Tell me who!*"

"Stop the games. I'm done. You should be, too. It'd do us both good."

Tony was chewing a mouthful of WAKE-UPZ. They tasted dry, chalky.

Tonight would be *his* night.

He had taken down the security cameras and mounted them on the inside of the supply room just outside of the beer cooler. Two monitors were up behind the counter. He could see every inch of the place in clear black and white. The video recorder was on in case he missed something, blinked.

There had been some rattling back there. Could have been anything: new inventory settling into place, mice eating into the two-week-old sacks of potatoes that were *still* on special for $2.99. *Are they ever going to take those away? They're just sitting there, rotting, festering. Christ, the stink. The manager, she could be in on this. That bitch. She has to know they're there; they must talk to her. They must!*

And the clinks, the clanks, the squeaks, that had all worked to their advantage before, whoever, or whatever, was back there, trying to push him clear over the edge. Not anymore. Their tiptoeing, their laughs at Poor-Fool-Tony, that was all ancient history. Things were about to change.

On the monitor, the cooler door looked like a black monolith. He waited for it to open, for a crack to appear, for the glowing light inside that lit up the fresh milk display to pour out. They were bold; they'd come out to take a peek, to see what he was up to. Last night, pink potpourri-scented detergent had been spilled in aisle two. Tony watched the tapes to see if he could spot them, the pool looking like blood on the grainy monitor image. But there was nothing. *They're trying to throw me off, confuse me. They know I'm on to them; that's it. They're scared. Yeah, scared. They're weak; I'm not. I'm strong.*

"*There!*" he screamed, pointing at the monitor, pressing his finger hard on the dirty glass surface, his face close. A sliver of light cut down the length of the door and reached out a foot into the darkness. *Could've been the air exchange. No, no, not now. They want me to see. It's a challenge. Those bastards!*

"I see you, *cunt!* I'll sleep soon."

Running, Tony took a box cutter to the back. He would have them in shreds before his shift was out, cut them up real nice and stuff them in the greasy dumpster with the inventory boxes where the cabbies liked to piss and get sucked off between jobs. Have them picked up by nine, by the disposal truck. Then he would go home and make her talk. She would talk, or he would spill her out across the kitchen floor. *I'll sleep like the dead, then. No more noise—just peace-and-fucking-quiet.*

He stepped into the supply room. He could hear them, faint and distant, moving around behind the door like a child's whisper during Sunday mass.

To hell with the games!

His foot to the door, he leapt in, wielding the box cutter, ready to strike, ready to cut and maim and amputate. But one step in, the floor dropped off. It had been completely erased, and he watched dust and gravel fall down into a dark abyss for what seemed like forever.

The place had somehow been transformed. Gone were the stacks of bottles, the dull and steady hum of the cooler's halogen lights. It had been a small concrete space, like a prison cell; now it was a deep and limitless cavern that reached back for miles, covered by sharp grey rocks and dotted on all sides with hundreds of small honeycomb caves. A black lake covered the expanse of the floor, and dark water rained down from the ceiling, high and untouchable, from some unseen river. It was hot here, too, humid, a thick and balmy heat, a dead heat.

This was an undiscovered place; this was the bowels of the Earth, something from Jules Verne.

"I know you're here," Tony yelled, his voice echoing a thousand times. "I'm tired." He pushed the blade of the box cutter up, the two clicks loud.

He could hear scuffing. Only a few of them, a half-dozen, maybe. Water rustled and splashed. *They're cautious. I'm a dangerous man, and they know it. That's why they hide.*

His eyes, heavy, scanned the cave. For a moment, shadows flashed and shifted and grew large, then receded back and grew large again.

They're coming.

Something nudged his foot. Tony looked down. Gripping the ledge was a nightmare thing. He stepped back and saw hundreds more like it clinging to the cave walls around him, a living, breathing carpet. Humanoid, hairless, their skin translucent, a squid's, he could see their insides working away like the cylinders of an engine, and their eyes, large and white and opaque, stared at him, unblinking.

Tony swung the blade in a wide arc. "I'll take you out, every last fucking one of you."

One of them fell from the ceiling, landing in front of him, squatted, ready to spring. It grunted something unintelligible, sounding guttural and wet, exposing a thousand needle teeth between blue lips. Then it stood. Its insides shifted, like a nest of snakes.

Tony swung again.

It grabbed his arm, gripping it like a vice.

"Jesus..." He tried to get at it, but it swatted his hand and the weapon fell.

They were all grunting in unison now, deafening: a laity in prayer.

The creature holding him held up its hand, palm out, exposing a slit, a vagina-like wound that sprouted a half-dozen eels. Withering, snapping, they reached for Tony.

Held tight, he tried to push back but couldn't. Then its hand was on his face, gripping it, smothering him. He could feel the eels slipping across his chin and cheeks, wet and slimy, searching for a way in, trying to squirm between his tight lips.

Breathing hard through his nose, huffing, he tried desperately not to open his mouth. Once in, who knew what they would do?

Another grabbed his head and hauled it back, prying his mouth open, a gaping hole. His tongue flopped, and he moaned. Then they were in, sliding down his throat, splashing around in his belly like fish in a bucket.

Then they were gone, slipping back out. Tony vomited and fell on his ass, pushing himself with his heels, hoping to get back to the store, the real world.

The creature stepped forward. "You can see now," it said, voice low and soft, a whisper. Gone were the groans and moans. "You'll see the world for what it really is, and then you will sleep."

Janet, his tormentor, had to be first. *She's the hump I have to get over.* Like they said: *Then you will sleep.* With her gone, the rest would come easy, quick.

He had expected tricks from her. Vague excuses and self-deprecation were her specialty; she was an expert. But he had prepared, steadied himself.

The air in the apartment tasted bad, like sulfur, like burned fish left on the pan. Janet was in on the bed sleeping, flaunting what he could not have. She had changed, her skin charcoaled and black, crusty and broken: a burn victim just hauled out of the smoldering ruins of some great conflagration. As he stood over her—the emergency axe from the store heavy in his hands, the blade unused, sharp—she opened her eyes. They were deep red, burned with hate.

She said something deep and guttural, monstrous, uninterruptible, spitting out a forked tongue.

Janet was gone. *Had there ever been a Janet? Was there always just this charcoaled husk, pretending to be Janet, pretending to be my wife?*

She knew what was coming. Arms went to cover her face, her hands claws, her nails butcher knives.

Making a snap at him, her teeth coming together like a bear trap, Tony brought the axe down on her chest. There was a cracking sound, and sparks flew out of her and up towards the ceiling, fireflies dancing. Hissing, the sheets stained in what looked like soot, she flailed and flopped around on the mattress, clutching desperately at the hole.

He pried the axe free and made another swing, taking her head off, sending ash spraying, smoke billowing out of the hole, like there was an incinerator piping deep within her belly. The fierce light in her eyes went out, her body silent and unmoving.

Standing there, watching, breathing, his eyes heavy with exhaustion, he waited for her to move. But after a few moments, there was nothing.

He wanted to crawl into the bed despite the Janet-thing, feel the cool sheets against his skin, let sleep overtake him, finally. *It's still dark out. It'd be easy. Just get in.*

But he still had work to do.

The manager was lying behind the counter, her body in two. The top looked normal, human, but her teeth were a shark's, rows of chainsaws ready to chew and gnash. Her bottom half had changed: black like Janet's.

Customers had been in and out, looking to check lotto tickets, picking up snacks for work, getting change. They hadn't seen a thing. And Tony had played his role, waiting until half past nine when the rush hour crowds had gone and he could finish up undisturbed.

"I told you that they would help."

Mopping, Tony looked up. Psoriasis was back, standing at the counter and looking over at the mess on the floor, his face no longer shifting and contorting.

"You'll sleep now. I told you they'd come to see you. I told you."

"What did they have *you* do?"

He held up his right arm. His hand was missing, replaced with a dark scabby stump. "It was causing me trouble. They suggested it should go."

"And you slept?" Tony asked, wringing out blood in a bucket.

"Of course. You will, too. And you have them to thank."

"They must want something in return."

"Just spread the word. That's it. That's all you have to do."

"Spread what? I don't—"

"They let you see the truth behind the lies of the world, Tony. You've seen; you know. Tell others like *us*."

Tony put the mop down and sat on two milk cartons stacked up next to the cigarettes case. "How will they know—I mean, how did they choose me?"

"You chose *them*, Tony. They just made themselves accessible. They're always there. Now finish up here and go home. Sleep."

The boy looked paranoid, confused—eyes bloodshot and fat. His movements behind the counter were quick and jittery.

Tony could tell right from walking in that the kid wasn't new: face pale, skin sallow. He picked at his skin like there was something crawling just beneath it, searching.

The sun hadn't come up yet. Customers were a half-hour away. Tony had time to talk, reason with him. "Morning," he said, walking up to the counter.

"Hey. Morning," the boy mumbled.

"Tired? Long night?"

"Yeah, can't wait to sleep."

Steady, slow. "Been waiting a long while for that, haven't you?" Tony had to be careful here. Too much too soon and there would be no telling how the guy would react.

"Excuse me?"

"Waiting for sleep. I used to work this racket, too. You can go weeks without a full night's sleep. I've heard some people go months, years even. Hope you're not one of those."

The kid smiled but looked hopeless, lost. "It's been a while. Feel like I'm in Dimension-Z sometimes. I ask the cabbies how they do it, and they just say that the body grows accustomed. Well, it isn't happening to me. My body's fucked."

"I hear that."

"Can I get you anything?"

Easy, nice, slow: "Nah, I'm here to talk."

"Talk?"

"I know how you can sleep. Sleeping is the easy part, once you get the work done."

"Man, what are you talking about?"

"Sleep. They're waiting back there, man. You just have to go see them. Then you'll sleep. Go back."

The boy's eyes got wild; his shoulders tensed. "Okay, I get it. Alright, this is the second fucking time this week." He reached down below the counter and brought up a lead pipe the size of a bat. "Get out of here before I take your head off!"

"Talk with them. Just go back there. You've heard them at night, haven't you?"

Making a furtive swing, a threat: "I haven't heard shit. Now fucking get out!"

Tony slammed his fists down on the lotto ticket case, cracking it. His hand came away bloody. "Listen, you don't understand—"

The clerk swung, hitting Tony square in the temple, tissue and blood spraying. He slumped to the floor mat, dark red pouring out his nose and mouth.

"Oh, Jesus..." The clerk ran around the counter and checked Tony's pulse. He knew before he even put his fingers to his neck that he was dead—the left side of Tony's head was cracked open, brain partially exposed, eyes still, staring and lifeless. "Oh, Christ, man... Fuck. *Fuck!*" Kneeling, the clerk clutched at his hair, sweating. It was the third time in as many weeks that he had been held up. He had decided after the last time that that was enough, that the next druggie to come in looking for money was going away with more than he'd bargained for.

If this had been back when he had first started, he might have listened to the guy, might have gone along with this craziness. It had been a hard slog adjusting.

No sleep can make you crazy, he thought, dialing 911.

Starved to Death

Byron was contracted by the powerful suits who made fortunes on the burgeoning fitness industry of the late 20th Century, the money behind the late-night gurus and infomercials promising ten-second abs and vanishing waistlines to tens of millions of Americans.

But with the Tony Littles and Suzanne Somers of the world fast becoming a dying breed, something new and visionary was in order. Something drastic had to be done.

Byron considered himself a little overweight. It was hard to stay in shape the way things were, not like when he was in the Army: toned, ripped, muscled, working like a well-oiled machine, when he'd eat raw goat to get by in the bush. Sitting, waiting, staring out the front window of his '86 Cadillac—the one with the extra-wide load—watching dust gather on the dashboard and candy wrappers collect on the seat turned him soft. His shirts were getting increasingly tight around his midsection; his pants strangled his groin. He tried to pass this off as a product of necessity, that he could get whipped back into shape whenever he wanted—it was only a matter of time and dedication.

The current job was supposed to run for just a few months. It stretched on for considerably longer. But it wasn't all that bad. His employers paid well, better than the local small-time crime lords with their extortion and torture jobs that he was accustomed to.

He waited for a few hours for Pricilla to come out of Wal-Mart. He was hired to monitor her. Not follow, *monitor*. She was in her early thirties, blonde, educated, average. She would be a catch if it weren't for her weight. She hadn't always been like that. No, she was once athletic, firm. But that was ten years, a few ruined relationships and two abortions ago. He knew these things because he was paid to know. He had her phone and home computer tapped, listened to her conversations, and followed her to work in the mornings and home again at night. He had been in her house, had gone through her things. She read trashy women's magazines, watched reality television.

Pricilla had been through every fad diet on the market, every exercise routine. She even had her stomach stapled—he saw pictures of the scars, hidden under her mattress, like a dark secret or a child's diary. Even with the surgery, even with a stomach one-fifth its normal size, she couldn't keep the weight off.

She finally emerged from Wal-Mart. He peered through his binoculars and saw that she had bought half a dozen bags of potato chips. He wrote it down in his logbook, snapped a few pictures.

Although he had never met Pricilla, he felt a certain amount of respect and admiration for her. She did more scratching and clawing than anyone he knew, even more than he did, yet she trudged forward and did not complain.

It was for that reason—the failures, not the trudging—that his employers had chosen her. She represented, to them, a new and untapped market.

It had to happen eventually. Not like his employers would just forget. No. They had it all planned for months. Years, maybe.

He arrived at the apartment late from his usual rounds—Pricilla had gone to a movie, alone—and found a plain unmarked manila envelope staring up at him from the rubber floor mat: instructions, procedures, pills. He was surprised it had taken them that long.

Byron sat at the kitchen table and read the letter, no more than a few sentences. Twenty-five grand, a deposit—all tens, twenties—was next to the ashtray: half now, half later. There was a key, too, beside the two small, unmarked plastic bottles.

The letter told him to get things in order. A date was listed. He was expected to take the subject and confine her for a specific duration of time, during which he was to carefully monitor her weight. The key was for a safety deposit box, which would be used to pick up refills. He was to give them to her in her food—microwave dinners, the cheap kind, the kind that are loaded with saturated fats, simulated sugars, and preservatives, the ninety-nine cent kind.

He put a match to the paper and let it burn in the ashtray, watched the dirty smoke curl up into the ceiling fan.

In the basement—not his place, an abandoned two-story on the lower east side—he went over a few last things. The floor was plain grey concrete, the walls exposed jip-rock and piping, the ceiling floor beams. It was dark, no windows. A single bare bulb lit the place. In the far right corner, he had built a small cell out of chain-link fencing, not much bigger than a prison cell. Restraints—thick chains and cuffs—were attached to an exposed pipe jutting out of the wall. There was a one-piece, lidless toilet and a mattress.

He locked the gate, snapped the cuffs to the pipe and made sure they'd hold. Starting tomorrow, this would be Pricilla's new home.

Assassination and murder were Byron's business. But he had considerable experience with kidnapping, torture and home invasion; he figured more than most in his line of work. He had something of a reputation within his circles. He figured that was why he was hired.

Day now. Morning. Pricilla was awake and chained to the pipe; she had been awake for some time. The hysterics were over, and she was relatively calm.

Byron stood behind the black shower curtain strung up along the ceiling beams. Using a broom, he slid a microwave dinner through to her cell. There was a cocktail of chemicals mixed in with it: tasteless, odorless.

(*Feed two pills to the subject with each meal—one green, one red. Monitor. Wait for further instructions.*)

On the security monitor, she stared at the tray. Through a cheap voice distorter, he told her she would be treated well. He wouldn't violate her or cause her any harm, but if she tried to escape, things would get unpleasant. He didn't want that. No, there was no need, since he would let her go in a few weeks, anyway.

She asked him why he did this.

Because he was paid to.

She asked who paid him; she could pay, too.

He told her she didn't have that kind of money.

With a remote, he switched on the television that was bolted to the ceiling just outside the cell and beyond her reach.

He left.

Chains rattled; more crying.

She'd been given a remote. Stations flicked as she searched for something on cable.

Byron found it amusing how the movies portrayed kidnapping. Women cried and begged, snotted and pleaded. Men said they had a family and that there was no reason to do this, but not much else. In his experience, men were the cowards, not the women. Men almost always got on their knees, as if in supplication, and tugged at the leg of your pants, pissed themselves. Women usually kept silent, like it was something they had been anticipating all their lives, like they had made peace with it long ago.

Pricilla was like that. After the first day, she rarely asked questions. She ate the food she was given. She was tough, tougher than a lot of the professionals he'd come across over the years: muscled, hulking dark men without necks, former boxers and linebackers, men who'd broken more legs than he'd care to count.

Add to that her sudden rapid weight loss. As per his instructions, she weighed herself each morning before breakfast with an electronic bathroom scale he pushed through. In a few days, she'd lost thirty pounds. He could see it in her face, looking at her grainy image on the monitor, and her clothes had started to hang off her hips like loose skin.

He'd received additional instructions in the mail. She was to be weighed three times a day now, not twice: before breakfast, before supper, before sleep.

As she shed the pounds, his own weight began to trouble him more than usual. *It's getting out of control*, he thought, his chest a saggy wave, stomach cut like a bag of milk. *It's the lack of exercise. I'm in the house all day, sitting around, doing nothing, slowing my metabolism to a virtual standstill.*

He stared at himself in the mirror, sometimes by the hour, standing in the bathroom in nothing but his boxers, feeling at his love-handles, inspecting his imperfections, pinching and grabbing at fat deposits along his thighs until they turned red and sore, wishing he had the balls to just take a kitchen knife to them and trim them off, skin and fat, have it done with.

Byron stood behind the curtain. "I'm to weigh you three times a day now." He pushed the scale through.

She was quiet.

"I've brought you supper, too." The springs in the scale creaked. "Pork chops, mashed potatoes, gravy and biscuits. It's a TV dinner, the usual." The stuff looked like sludge, seventeen hundred and fifty calories that would go right to cellulite.

Low, emotionless: "275."

Another ten pounds since the night before last. If things kept up, she'd be rail-thin in another week; she'd look like something out of Auschwitz, a skeleton with eyes, maybe, breasts gone, cheeks sunken in, unable to stand without assistance.

Pricilla ate her food and watched television like she was supposed to. Despite the pain, she bided her time and waited patiently.

She wasn't stupid. She wasn't some frail little thing. She had plans and schemes of her own. She let *him* think she was compliant. *Whatever's in that food is going to get me out of here*, she told herself, swallowing in hard, forced gulps, feeling it sit in her gut like wet cardboard.

Her stomach had receded, and her knees and back ached less. She was sure her breasts were several sizes smaller. Her clothes—dirty, sweat-stained—no longer fit. The fat was just falling off. She was the lightest she had been since high school.

But a deep hunger gnawed at her. No matter what he slid over, she was never full and always starving. At night, she woke clutching her stomach, buckling into a fetal position as sharp stabbing pain shot across her midsection and up through her chest. Then there was a blinding whiteness. Her heart would pump fast and hard and mean. All she could do was bite down on the pillow, not wanting *him* to hear her, not wanting to show signs of weakness.

The handcuffs were getting loose enough so that they no longer pinched her wrists and cut into the skin, but far too tight to slip out of.

Soon, though. Soon.

Pricilla watched intently as the rat picked through the spilled food just outside the cell: microwave spaghetti, just noodles and stinking sauce. The rat had become a regular, having come by the last two days looking for scraps.

The man felt that her diet needed change. Still undercooked, still tasting like dog meat, still slimy and rubberized in her mouth, she ate it the first few times. At least the man had done that for her. He was breaking whatever guidelines he'd been following. It was more than she expected from him, and a good sign. But once she started to get sick, violently sick, far sicker than before— dark red viscous streaks mixed in the vomit on the floor, in the toilet—she stopped. Her stomach had cramped up bad; each time it felt like her abdominal muscles were being wrung down a washboard.

The food was now grey and solidified. The rat didn't seem to mind.

There was something instinctive, primal, fierce bubbling up to the surface of her consciousness. Something foreign. And eyeing the rat, licking her lips, she thought of the South American tribe she'd seen on television who considered them a delicacy.

Just reach out through the bars. Grab it. Only a rat. You'll feel better when you eat; you'll be able to keep going. No poison in him.

Pricilla got down off the cot and onto her knees, slowly crawling towards the bars, breathing slow, easy, not wanting to startle it.

For a second, it looked back over its shoulder, sensing danger, nose twitching.

Slipping her free hand through the bars, easy, the other taut and stretched out to the limit, she snatched the rat up in one quick motion, fast, like a snake. Hauling it back, it thrashed and squirmed, squeaked and tried to bite.

131

Pricilla squeezed hard with both hands. There was a muffled crunch, and the rat went limp.

Holding it by the head and hind legs, she bit deep into its belly and wrenched off a wet piece of meat, swallowing it down.

Then the hunger receded for a moment, for a tiny precious moment.

Had a day passed since eating the rat...?

Weeks...?

Since she stopped watching the television, Pricilla had no idea of time.

She was vomiting every half hour, screaming and clutching her stomach, her insides scraped of fat with surgical precision. She was the size of a marathon runner now, smaller, bones poking out beneath skin, ribcage a xylophone, shirt wet, a death shroud, hips too narrow to keep her pants up.

Byron could see that getting up on the scale had taken the good from her. She hadn't moved much since.

150. ONE HUNDRED AND FIFTY FUCKING POUNDS! Solid red digits blared out from the scale like flashing hazard lights.

"I'm starving. Hungry..." she moaned, rocking, arms hugging her chest, eyes wide and fixed at an unseen spot on the floor.

"What can I get you?" Byron asked. He would feed her whatever she wanted. She just had to say it.

For a moment, silence. Nothing from the cage but heavy panting. Then: "It don't matter..." she moaned. "It don't matter..."

She was going into shock. He had to keep her awake, conscious. She'd probably die if she slept—it had gotten that bad. "You've done good, Pricilla. There's just another few days left. Hang on. I'll let you go then, like I promised. Get you to a hospital," he said, trying to calm her, but sounding small, impotent. She wasn't lasting that long—a day or two at most.

A whisper: "So... hungry..."

"I know. Eat some of the food I brought down. Please. You'll feel better."

The tray was at her feet. The food was cold now, solidified, a rock, reheated twice already. She wouldn't touch it.

"Hungry..."

She had that pale and sweaty look of defeat about her. It was an impressive spectacle, though, watching her like this, holding on. Harder men would have buckled. But there was something fierce and dangerous in her eyes, something he hadn't seen in a long time, something that even she probably had no idea existed, something Byron had only seen in animals of men, men determined to commit violence, criminals, men who spent their lives incarcerated or fighting in foreign wars.

With nothing left in it, Pricilla's stomach was making a low grinding noise, twisting, knotting up. With each fresh rumble, there was a stiff pain deep in her extremities, like cancer. She was convinced that her stomach, her cannibal stomach, was eating her alive. Where else had the fat receded to?

Her mind was on replay. *No dying here. No. Won't let that happen. Not here. That's not how it's supposed to end. Not like this. Not lying in some cage, an animal.*

She'd been patient, waiting for the pounds to drop like he had said they would. They had. Too many pounds. Pulling and tearing at the cuffs, an hour of it, kicking, screaming, crying, had produced little. Depression had set in: heavy, overwhelming, forcing her down.

Get out. Do whatever has to be done. She listened to that inner voice for a while, looked at the cuffs, her wrists. Then she chomped down on her wrist with no inhibitions and tore out a juicy chunk of meat. Her wrist was ragged, teeth-marked and bloody, all raw meat, bone exposed. But no pain, just numbness. Blood running down her chin, it looked like she'd dipped it in red. Tasting the sharp coppery taste of it, spitting it to the floor, she bit down again, this time a mouthful, her cheeks almost stuffed.

Cuffs still tight, looking down at her wrist, blood running out in a free flow, thick, making a puddle on the concrete, she felt floating, light, then spinning. Her mouth open, chewed-up muscle hanging out, she fell back, unconscious.

Lights on. Lights off. Dimmed. As bright as they could go. Reading lamp on the floor by his feet, like at a runway or bodybuilding competition. He placed it at varying angles and then removed the shade. Flexing. Posing. Hoping the artificial light would reveal a newly developed muscle, a fresh vein popped to the surface, a striation, possibly. Standing, hands on the mirror, sweat dripping from his sides, his body looked the same: round, curved, sagged, stomach protruding over the tight elastic of his boxers.

It's like a woman's. Like a goddamn woman's.

Byron inspected himself after each workout, with self-hatred and disgust, checked for progress, but was always dissatisfied, like now. Each month, he'd intensify his training regimen: another exercise, increased repetitions, pushups, abdominal crunches, calisthenics, like when he was in the Army, jumping-jacks until his ankles were sore.

It calmed him, his training, let him think. That's why he'd come up from the basement: to get his thoughts straight, get his head around things.

Something had to be done about Pricilla. He'd watched the poor girl suffer for six months through a high-powered zoom lens, listened to her mother through the wire-tap, her sister from Vermont, her brother in Tallahassee, listened to their scratchy voices and vile talk about the way *she* was and how *she* lived her life. He wasn't going to let things continue on their current path. *Couldn't.* And to hell with his employers. He had other plans.

Waking, body on autopilot, brain on fire, a searing heat ran through her, emanating from her belly like an oil furnace, which made her crazy and desperate.

Already, the hunger gnawed, raped her insides, chewed away at her gut with sharp gnashing teeth.

She smacked the wall—sweating—slammed the steel handcuffs against the concrete in a barrage. The wall chipped and spat dust. Crying, cursing incoherently, she broke her hand, snapped the bone. Bracing her feet against the pipe, hauling, pulling against the cuffs, straining, shaking, thrashing, crying, she finally slipped out, like a hard birth.

Mind racing, her eyes darted to every corner, every inch of the place. She knew only escape: a loud neon billboard in her mind.

Wild, crazed, she shook the door, screaming, pushing. It heaved out. Kicking at the lock, driving her heel down into it, her feet became bloody shoes, leaving red prints on the floor.

Pain swelled and buckled her again, clutched her abdomen with strong hands.

Wailing, desperate, she fell to the floor.

Weak...

Panting...

Like a wounded animal.

Slouched against the fence, seeing the wet handcuffs, the pipe twisted out from the wall, she grabbed it, pulled hard until it finally cracked and fell to the floor with a dull clank.

She picked it up and beat it across the padlock, snapping it. The gate swung open.

Above her, movement.

Someone... *The man?*

Then, remembering him, his voice, loud, and visualizing the tray pushed through the curtain, begging her to eat, pleading with her, she knew she hated him, knew he was killing her.

She gripped the pipe with both hands and waited.

Things had changed, become grey; he was used to black and white. He could finish the job. That was easy enough: a bullet to the back of the head was only a matter of pulling a trigger, a jerk of the index finger. Simple. But he hadn't anticipated that dreaded thing assassins fear like the plague, the thing that must be vanquished without reproach or self-recrimination: sympathy. It crept into your body like a disease, an incurable virus. It warped your brain, destroyed your senses.

Down the narrow stairs, the rank smell of human waste and spoiled food was thick: poison gas. Choking: "You're going home. They've got their results, and I don't want what they've paid me for."

Pushing a blindfold through the shower curtain: "Put this on."

Nothing. Silence from the other side.

"Take the blindfold, Pricilla."

Still nothing.

Sounding firm: "Pricilla?"

He went to the monitor.

The door to the cell was half-open, the lock smashed. Cuffs bloody, pipe gone, ripped from the wall, the stained mattress was unoccupied. No Pricilla.

Reaching for the baton in the desk, finding it, cold and black, snapping it open with a flick of his wrist, he hoped he wouldn't have to use it. "You want to go home, right, Pricilla?"

There was the wet slap, slap, slap of bare feet on concrete.

Running.

On instinct, Byron spun, raised the baton.

Too late. *Too slow.*

He was hit. Face instantly numb. Blinding flashes. Ears buzzing loud, deafening, like white noise. Dizzy, unbalanced, he fell to his knees, arms up to protect himself. Hit again: back of the head. Face suddenly warm and wet, he was struck again, even harder, the white turned black.

Pricilla sat on the floor in an ever-expanding pool of blood, Byron's limp body draped over her lap—eyes dead and staring, mouth fish-gaping. His shirt torn off, she'd opened him up, arms buried up to the elbows in gore, hauling out whatever she could get her hands on. Loops of guts were strung out around her, his torso a vacuous and dark space. Her cheeks puffed out like a gluttonous child, she moved her jaw in slow and deliberate movements, savored the meat.

He'd been a big man, and there was still a lot to eat.

Belly hard and full, barely able to stuff any more of him into her, she swallowed in a forced gulp, the hunger raging, burning her blood, compelling her to eat even more. Bits of chewed liver fell from her mouth.

She undid his belt and tugged at his pants. His white legs were thick, hard muscle behind fat.

"Starving..." she mumbled, licking her lips and digging in for seconds.

Dancers in the Dark

I t was once the base camp for the Blue Coal Company. Clarksville.

A small isolated community in eastern Kentucky, a day's drive from the nearest town and five miles off the interstate. Just a patch of a half-dozen dark and sagging gum and paper thatched shacks. Past the stripped, barren, flood wasted ghost-town trailer park that even the hippie squatters wouldn't set down in. The only road leading up, crushed rock and dirt, was barely a road at all.

The Collins and Napier families were content in this isolation, feared change, despised outsiders.

Doc Sam knew the road well. He had taken over from the company doctor and had been treating the two families for the better part of three decades, three generations, and knew the tragedies, floods, violent deaths, and sicknesses that had cut them down, erased the Crows, who were themselves now memory, anecdotes from past bad years.

Standing up in the living room, shirtless, thumbs hooked in his belt-loops, hopping from boot to boot, Brice Collins asked nervously, "She'll be alright, won't she?"

It was something Doc Sam dreaded but had heard before many times. He mopped his considerable forehead and stared at the patch of discolored and twisted skin at the pit of Brice's stomach, which looked like a knot, where his

139

brother John, a mean drunk, now dead from tuberculosis and buried behind the house, had blasted him open with a shotgun. Brice displayed his scar with pride and often talked of his brother with affection. "I don't know. The baby's breached. They both might die. It would've been best if we'd have gotten her to a hospital. But she won't last that long now, I don't think. Not in my car, anyway. They'll be dead before we hit the road."

Brice considered this for a moment, picked at a crusty scab on his left elbow, kept his eyes fixed on the floor. "Can't you just cut it loose?"

"I'll have to."

She was quiet now, Maggie, unconscious on a small cot in the back room, her chest rising slower all the time, her breath shallow, skin pale and sweaty, cold.

"She's in a real bad way. You'll have to make a decision now, Brice. You're the father."

He put his hands back through his long, slick hair, dyed black with shoe polish. "Just get it done then. I'll tell her mother and get her over right off."

Doc Sam went to his bag, tattered brown leather, his initials embedded in gold below the latches. Turning to Brice, voice quick: "Go get me some fresh towels and water, too."

He took a rusted dinner tray from a pile of junk that had collected against the back wall, went into the room, unrolled a white towel from the bag. Wrapped inside were scalpels and clamps and various surgical instruments, cleaned and ready.

Maggie stirred, moaned. If she woke, he could do little for the pain. Without even chloroform, he feared that most.

There were sixteen babies buried up on the hill, close to the mine, all delivered by him. It was a heavy burden he accepted but never relished. He was an old man, and they had been wearing him down for years and would soon break him. A fresh bottle of Wild Turkey was under the sink at home, the seal unbroken. He'd put a dent in it tonight, drink until his throat was raw and his kidneys screamed blue murder.

He set up beside the cot, rolled up his sleeves.

The humidity in the room was choking and pungent; the sky had been threatening rain for days now. He could smell the rot of the walls, reminding him of tuberculosis and yellow fever.

This was where he did all his work, the only place they allowed any kind of treatment, and for him a place of bad memories. In the far right corner was a neat stack of dolls, dirty faces and soiled hair, blank staring eyes and false smiles—the toys of dead children, children he had treated. The walls were lined with black-and-white photographs, unframed, photographs of black-faced miners, soldiers, weddings, baptisms, births. A makeshift shelf, uneven, held dozens of glasses and teacups. Sam had looked in them once; they were filled with gold teeth, rings, ceramic eyes: icons.

He could hear the children playing in the dirt out front, barefoot, chasing one of the bitch dogs with sticks, laughing, many of them without parents, siblings. They were singing something about singing birds and loving mothers.

Bringing her dress up to her breasts, he put his stethoscope to her belly and listened, held his breath.

He swallowed hard then pressed his fingers into her womb, felt for the baby. A shudder went through him. He knew what he would find.

He'd have to be quick.

Brice's boots banged off the floorboards, shaking the house. "Take these. Best I could do," he said, huffing. "Her mother's on her way."

Doc Sam turned and saw Brice had brought an armful of linen—some stained, some clean and white. "They'll have to do," he said, lips pursed, taking them. "I have to get started. Her mother will have to wait."

Doc Sam folded two sheets, put them around the incision area, just above her navel, and another at the foot of the bed to wrap the baby in. "You'll have to leave. I can't have distractions. If anything happens, I'll holler."

He pushed Brice out, closed the door. Locked it. He could hear the boy move to the front stoop, yelling at someone: Maggie's mother, probably.

Kneeling beside the bed, he took the scalpel, stared at her belly for a moment, steadied his hand, and made a short vertical incision. Thick red blood pooled up. It smelled of copper and leaked down her side and across her sharp milky hips, quickly soaking the sheets. Holding the hole open with two small clamps, he cut into her uterus, reached inside for the baby. Taking it by the ankles, he lifted it out and into the world. The dark, coiling umbilical cord dangled down into the hole. The baby was quiet, still, unmoving. It did not cry; oxygen would never fill its lungs with life. It was not breathing; he was glad for that, glad for Maggie.

Barely human, he didn't try to revive it. Its right arm was just a stub, thalidomide-like, its skull far too large and overdeveloped on the right side, dragging its head down towards its shoulder. Heavy blue veins snaked across its forehead. Feet fused together, its legs were thin, bony. It could never hope of living in this world.

He cut the cord and wrapped the baby in one of the sheets. It was a small, frail bundle.

Sighing deeply, tears ran down his face, mixed with sweat.

Maggie was a child herself—he guessed sixteen at most—far too young to bear children. He wondered if she knew what had moved and shifted inside of her, knew what it looked like, and if she ever could've loved it.

Her face was so handsome and still; she could have been sleeping. But her chest was flat and unmoving, dead. A hospital was what she had needed, not him. He was good for measles and stitches and a case of gout, but not much else.

Brice was cursing to be let in, banging at the door, and Doc Sam could hear the children still chasing the dog, whipping and swatting at it, singing loudly, a chorus now.

Tonight would be hard for him. Stillbirths always were. They haunted him, came to him in his dreams like a thief in the night, but he didn't have much left for them to take. Not much at all.

The blisters on his hands had been torn open for some time. Digging since dawn, the exposed flesh was raw and pink and wet. He'd wrapped his hands in his filthy socks; that hadn't helped. "Put her down nice. Don't go dropping them," Brice said, holding the rope tight. Even with the two of them in the box, dangling a few feet in the grave, the weight light, his back was ready to break.

Maggie's brother Cecil was on the other side, feet dug deep into the grass. Beneath his sagging white shirt, soiled and sweaty, his ribs clearly visible, he looked all spent and wasted. "I won't go dropping nothing," he replied. The tall grass swayed in a wave around the rusted debris, making him anxious. His eyes darted, scanned the edge of the clearing, the tree line, searching for something unseen. "I don't feel right up here. Men don't belong up here."

"Then let's get it done."

They lowered the box into the ragged hole, and it hit the bottom with a soft thud.

"We should say something. A prayer or something."

Brice grabbed a spade stuck into the small mound of earth beside the grave and starting pitching dirt. "No prayers. None of that up here, all right? It's going to rain soon; they won't need any of that."

"She was my sister."

The grease of his hair left dark sweat-streaks across his face. "And she was my woman, boy. Don't forget my daughter's in there with her."

The clouds to the east looked dark like iron, a winter sky creeping towards them. Rain would be coming soon. Heavy rain. The Monongahela River coursed and pulsed beneath them. It overflowed sometimes, filling the mine and spewing forth, spitting out old trolleys, pickaxes, tables, lamps, and whatever else the Blue Coal Company had left behind, leaving a long trail of debris. It had reached the town only once. That had been a year after the Great War, a year after the company had hauled out. The old woman Crow was the first to go, to get sick, balloon up and dry out like a cyst, and the rest of her clan soon followed. They were buried just below the hill and drowned in lime, their shack boarded up, encased like a tomb and burned down. The old maids would tell tales that the woman could be heard moaning up on the hill, searching through the brush, starved, hunting wild game, crying for her children.

The two men filled the hole quickly.

Cecil patted the fat pimple of raw earth. "We'd best get. This place isn't for us. It's no good."

"Don't worry about nothing. This is a good thing, Cecil. They're good here. Better than before. They're with family. But you're right; this isn't a place for a man to be."

Maggie...? Is that you?

You shouldn't be out this time of night with just a nightgown on. You'll freeze; remember the baby. It's not so good to be out in this when you're carrying. And you're rotten, woman! Mud all over yourself; soaked to the bone.

Does Brice know you're out? If you don't want a licking, you'd best get down to the house. Fast, too.

I know. I know.

Happy? I'm glad; real glad.

Sure, I like music. Can't dance, though.

All right, just this once. Brice won't like it a bit if he finds us up here.

Digging for what?

He bolted upright, still at the kitchen table. Pasted to the linoleum tablecloth, his face ached.

He'd been dreaming, dreaming the dreams of *them* again: Clarksville, and now Maggie, too.

God! Maggie...

Sun was pouring into the kitchen from the window above the sink and through the blinds, cutting the table, the half-drained quart of whiskey, the overflowing ashtray, into dark slices.

The radio clock blared at him with its red accusatory eyes. *8:15. Jesus! Been here all night.*

A sudden blinding pain shot down from the crown of his skull to his temples. He went to the cupboard above the fridge and got two aspirin, washed them down with a quick slug from the bottle, winced, took another, gargled, spit it into the sink, and stood staring into the dark drain-hole.

They'd bury Maggie today, then the baby. Brice probably already had them in the ground.

He picked up the phone, dialed the number he always dialed when he found himself like this.

It rang five times before a surly voice answered.

"Jason?" he started. "I didn't wake you, did I?"

The voice on the other end sounded groggy, sleepy, still half-cut, and sluggish. "No. No. I was just getting up. The dogs are yowling to be fed."

"Late night?"

"Too late."

"Me, too."

He could hear the click of a lighter, the long drag off of a cigarette. "So what's up?"

Flat, monotone: "Maggie's dead. The one I saw yesterday. So is her baby: stillbirth. Not much I could do. The thing was wasted away. Something genetic, I'd say. Terrible stuff. But in some ways a blessing."

A whisper: "Christ..."

"They'll have them buried today. That's two this year."

A dead pause went out over the line and seemed to hang there forever.

"You alright, Sam?"

"Can't say I am."

"Anything I can do?"

"Just thought I'd call and inform you, make it legit and all. I'll file the papers tomorrow."

"Take your time. You know, if I had something to show the Health Board, I don't know, something to prove to them the kind of things you have to deal with, we might be able to force them to get something done about Clarksville. Not so much for the men, but for the women and the kids. But I doubt they'll go out of their way for a bunch of hillbillies. Never have; probably never will."

Sam considered this for a moment. The aspirin had barely put a dent in his headache, and it was now cutting down into his neck and shoulders. Kneading them: "What do you mean?"

"I don't know. Get her an autopsy or something."

"Christ, no! Those women are lucky they've had even me. Besides, I'm done with that now. I'm done. I've done all I *can* do."

"I understand. You know I'm here for you, buddy. Come in to the office when you get a chance and fill out the forms. No rush. We'll get ourselves drunk while we're at it; shoot the shit."

"Will do."

"By the way, they give that baby a name? Christened?"

"No. No name. None of that. They don't allow it."

Sam could hear the clink of glass as ice cubes hit the bottom of a tumbler. Jason had lost his wife the year before last. Cancer had eaten her up, and he was prone to the bottle and was known as an earlier drinker. He'd be full by noon. "They say that un-christened babies go to limbo. Mama didn't have me christened, and my brothers used to say it to torment me. Used to scare the shit out of me." He threw the drink back with a distinct gulp, forced a laugh.

"Listen to me. I'm talking shit. I'd best get going. Don't forget to drop by, and I'll see you soon, buddy."

"Yeah. Soon." He hung up the phone.

It was cold, his breath icy, the rain-soaked trees drenching his clothes.

He crossed the slick rope bridge, never looking down, the river raging, surging beneath him, and climbed the soft embankment leading up to the mine, which he knew overlooked the graveyard but had never seen.

The rain had been heavy and wild and had only just let up, turning the ground, the path, to mud, parts swallowing his rubbers, sucking him down into the earth. But Clarksville had been spared: no flashflood, no mudslide. The worst had diverted into the Monongahela.

Peering into the brush, the flashlight barely piercing the blackness, he felt used up, spent. It was a hard go, hard to catch his breath, fill his lungs, and not meant for an old man. Besides the road leading up from town, and all that was left to the company's trolley tracks, this was the only way he knew. Brice was unstable, a little gone and violent, often quick to use his rifle. He would have surely turned on Sam if he knew his intentions.

Sitting in his blue '56 Ford Vic, beaten and worn and rusted, neglected, the back seats sagging and covered in junk, the radio off and parked behind two trailers, Sam had considered these things as he watched the night slowly take hold, the rain lash at the windshield for an hour, maybe two, listened, let his hands roam over his bag instinctively, like there was some secret written in Braille on the surface that only he knew existed and could decipher, constantly opening it to assure himself his instruments were there, that all he needed to do was get out of the car. Everything else would take care of itself.

Maggie's wasted face, her young face, stayed with him, imprinted on his brain like the Photostat copy of Jesus—

the pained and crucified Jesus—that hung behind the grocery counter and continued to amaze and transfix children who stared at it long enough.

Jason, drunk, crying, a few drinks between old friends quickly turning into a late night binge, held up off the interstate in the Super 8 where Sam had left him, his wife dead two years to the day, said that he was the cruelest bastard he knew. Gripping Sam by the shoulders, half-naked and greasy-looking: "You're good. You're a good friend, Sam. But I'm not good like you. I wasn't good when she needed me. I know that. Those women, they need you, boy. Christ, do they need you."

Sam's knees shook with exhaustion. He was weary. Another fresh quart of Wild Turkey was in the glove compartment, waiting. He wished to good-goddamn he could take a long haul off it now to numb himself, feel his throat burn. But he needed clarity up here, needed to feel like he was still among the living, not the wretched things Jason had become: face a dark mask of anxiety, prematurely aged and dying inside.

The crest of the hill was just up ahead, the hazy yellow beam of the flashlight tracing the end of the path. Between the trees, he could see the white chalk face of the hill rising up into the night. Hidden deep within the clouds, the moon was a luminescent shadow, barely visible, making the mine, buried and boarded up, just a dark mound pushing out from the rock.

He moved forward, wet tree branches slapping his face, his Army-issue shovel clanking.

At the top, he took a deep breath, his lungs aching. The grassy plateau slowly declined to the west, and the path vanished under the brush. He could see a rusted out trolley on its side, looking like a dead animal, a horse. A piece of track was partially buried by his foot, splintered and rotten with decay.

The wind began to pick up again, freezing his legs, whipping the grass, carrying with it a ripe stink. He thought he could hear talking, whispering, from somewhere beyond the trees.

Brice...!

The boy was probably pissed, more pissed than he'd ever been pissed, cursing every bloody name he could. Doc Sam pictured him barely conscious, covered in mud from clawing at the ground, sprawled out by Maggie's grave with a .410 cocked-n-ready, his wife and child splayed out next to him.

Sam turned off the flashlight, moved slowly, carefully down the hill.

There were other voices and laughter. His cousin was probably down there with him, just as drunk, dancing around, singing into his bottle until Brice fired off a blast in his general direction.

On his haunches, down beneath the branches, he crawled forward, knees creaking. He could see a flicker of light, a fire licking up into the sky, spitting sparks. Shadowy figures, silhouettes, danced around it, singing arm-in-arm.

He went to the edge of the thicket. Moving a branch, he peered out.

His heart leapt into his throat, tasting like hot bile or battery acid, and he squatted down.

All he knew as a man of science—the limbic system, biology, firing neurons, death, oxygenated red blood cells— was dashed away at that moment, erased. His head swirled, and he was a child again, weak in the dark, helpless like Jason had become. It was a horrible spectacle, some Grand Guignol dance troupe of the dead. Between the upturned mounds of grave dirt, dirty children, their tiny bodies eaten away with decay, danced and hopped and skipped through the grass and around the fire, playing. They were singing, their voices rasping, ugly and metallic. And he knew the song; he'd heard it sung the day before. A few more held squirming, shrieking fetus dollies, combed out stringy mud-crusted hair. The boys, one with no arms or legs, hopped on stumps, played tag.

(Jared! That's his name. I remember him. Stillborn; mother dead, too. But that was two summers ago.)

Women, a few obviously mothers, a half-dozen of them, sat on upturned carts, trolleys, talking, smiling, laughing.

He recognized some, what was left of them. They'd been treated for TB, syphilis, and the children smallpox, diphtheria. A few had died while giving birth, the children stillborn. All of them had been patients of his; he was as sure of this as the hand in front of him was his. He knew he could go home, pull out their charts in his office, read the few notes he'd made, the medications he'd prescribed, the death certificates he'd filed.

But there were no men to speak of, dead or alive.

It could have been a card party, a child's birthday, but the light of the fire revealed skull faces, flapping skin, black hole eyes, clumps of twisting worms and curling maggots hiding behind ears, burrowing in for the last morsel of dead meat. And the stench, sweet and sick and thick in the air, made him want to vomit.

Several women were gathered around a mother cradling her baby. She was thin and wasted, but her skin was whole, fresh, not like the others. She turned for a moment, and Doc Sam saw that it was Maggie. The bulbous head of her child sucked eagerly at her deflated and sagging breast. The hole he had made with his scalpel hung open, her guts looping out and reaching the grass.

She was smiling, happy to be with her newborn child.

They were all happy.

This was a celebration, he realized. Of life. Not death.

And his heart was finally glad.

The Last Highwayman

"**S**plit the bitch in two," Mack laughed, picking a piece of tobacco from between his rotten teeth. He watched with excitement at Henry's sweaty grin and his hips coming down, down, his pants around his ankles.

Naked, arms and legs splayed out like a crucifixion, bound at the hands and ankles to thick stakes, tongue cut out, her skin was bruised and bloody and torn and burned-up from exposure. The two shootists had been raping her for days; Jeremiah wouldn't have any of it, figuring that if she didn't give it up willingly, it wasn't worth having.

Her man was gone, eaten over four meals.

Lost in the wastelands for two months, hunting a bounty, the three assassins got violence on the mind. Emerging from the dry, blasting heat, half-crazed, setting camp by the roadside, their mules devoured a month ago, they waited a week for a car to pass.

Lips cracked, thin and wasted, the rusted-out Buick was a godsend. It'd come over the horizon with dark smoke billowing out from beneath the hood, the exhaust firing shots out the back, and died by the side of the road in a hissing heap. Dead-sick with radiation poisoning, a man and women were slumped over the front seat.

Now, with the radiator patched up, Jeremiah wanted to push on, try for the outposts, follow the few leads they still had on the General, pick him up as he emerged out of the desert.

The three of them were exposed out here, without any *real* shelter to speak of. And Jeremiah knew that it was by pure luck that they had avoided the windstorms, mutants, the packs of starved savage desert dogs that roamed along the highway. But Henry and Mack wanted to stick it out, wait and see what came next. Maybe there was an exodus out of the colony; there'd be more meat then, a better rig.

Jeremiah sat on the large fist-like rock poking up from the desert floor, considered his options as he watched Henry finish with a grunt and wipe himself on her belly.

Zipping up, Henry said, "I'd say she's spent. Not much to her now but eats. She might even be dead. I can't tell."

Jeremiah cracked his sawed-off .30-30 and placed a dirty slug in the empty barrel.

Not right in the head, Mack danced around, kicked sand up, and squealed in excitement.

Even if she was alive, she wouldn't last more than a week. Her eyes were swollen shut and puffed out like dirty bruised apples; blood ran from between her legs in a steady stream. She was rotten with lung cancer, her face covered in a dark viscous fluid that she'd been coughing up since they'd found her.

Without considering it twice, Jeremiah brought the hammer back and pulled the trigger. There was a sharp, thunderous clap and her head was instantly erased, leaving a dark, messy streak spread out across the sand and a ragged hole at her neck. Her body made several quick jerking motions and was still.

Sniffing at the cordite, thick and coppery in the air, Mack laughed, licking his chops. "Don't you love that smell? Means food. Makes me hungry."

Reloading and holstering his weapon, and knowing he'd have to kill these two if he was to get to an outpost, Jeremiah said, "I won't eat no woman-meat."

The sun slipped below the horizon before they got to supper.

Jeremiah waited patiently.

The sky painted in a red-orange haze like an A-bomb had gone off over some distant city, he watched them cook her on a spit and eat her, their chins dripping with grease. Buzzards, bold and brazen, cawed and picked at the heap of undistinguishable mess they'd scooped out of her stomach and left in a shallow pit to burn. The smell was bad, worse than even tough donkey meat. It reminded him of war.

Watching them turn the hot meat over in their mouths, steam coming out, disgust quickly billowing up in him, he opened them up in two quick shots. Henry had a tunnel running straight through his chest and was dead before he hit the dirt. Mack wailed and clawed at the blast-hole in his side, which Jeremiah could see straight through, and tried desperately to keep his guts in, dancing around and spitting half-chewed meat.

Gathering up the supplies, Jeremiah got in the Buick and drove off in a puff of black smoke, leaving Mack to the buzzards.

"Half a gallon of water and some boots is the best I can do," the man said, half his face riddled with the cyst scars and lumps familiar to the war generation. The squat little garage was filled with rusted heaps of car parts, greasy engine blocks, tires piled against the walls. It'd been a job to get the Buick in. "With that radiator, I'm being generous."

He was right. After two months and seven outposts, following a dozen leads that never amounted to much, this was Jeremiah's first taker. The radiator was split and bleeding from a hundred places, another dozen plugged up and ready to burst. A half-dead mule he'd picked up off a trader in New Omaha had dragged it here. He extended his hand. "Deal."

"Come back tomorrow morning and I'll have those boots. One's got to be mended."

Jeremiah's gut hurt, and he was dead weak. The last thing he'd eaten was the leather off his right shoe, and he'd lost two teeth trying. "Anywhere I can get a decent meal?"

"Across the road. Tell Sally I sent you. She'll expect something, but not much."

Jug of water slung over his shoulder, he gathered up his things from the back seat.

Outside, the sun had drawn back behind the clouds, and there was a piss-yellow windstorm brewing, lurking dangerously off the horizon like a dark tidal wave. The streets were barren. Everyone had gone below ground. Mutants usually came in with the storms, starved.

The town, nameless, wasn't much of a town, much of anything, just another outpost lying on the edge of the wasteland, a place for stragglers and vagabonds. Tilting, windowless grey shacks lined the roads, probably filled with the same flash-burnt faces and blind men, crab-clawed children and barren women.

Radioactive dust had collected in heaps in the gutters. Almost picked clean, gums peeled back into a grin, his mule lay dead on the road, covered in a sea of buzzing black flies. He felt at its poking ribs. Patches of skin had already been eaten away, the rest ready to slough off, not leaving much. Jeremiah cursed himself for not killing it weeks ago; the meat might have been good then. There was another body that he hadn't noticed before. Heavy with decay, he had obviously taken the worst of a gunfight. His shirt flapped in the wind and was riddled with bullet holes. He'd been stripped of his boots and jacket.

Sally's house was a two-level shack, the front door covered in a thin sheet of grey aluminum. He knocked and went in. It was rank with the stink of human waste and dead meat. Thin shafts of dull light came through the tightly boarded-up windows. He could make out sagging ancient furniture and crooked portraits on the walls.

Heavy boots clanked on the floor, and the hallway was suddenly flooded with light. "Can I help you?" a woman asked. "What business you got here, mister?"

Sally, Jeremiah figured. She was short and hunched and wore a soiled and tattered dress. Her face was covered in a hood. Most women, women old enough to know what the world had been like before the bombs and still felt pride and shame, often wore them to hide deformities. "I'm looking for boarding. A night, maybe two. I can pay."

"What have you got to offer?" Her voice was coarse, like she'd eaten sand.

"Quart of water."

"Two nights, eh?" She licked her immense balloon lips, blackened and blast-scorched. Jeremiah hadn't had a woman in five years and wanted one badly, but not bad enough to want her. "Alright. Room in the back is free. I got one other boarder upstairs. Been here for a week. Real quiet; he won't bother you none."

She took him to a dirty little back room, wallpaper curled up from the baseboards, bare besides a stained mattress, rusty cot and an overflowing piss-pot that was surrounded by a sea of scuttling cockroaches. The wind ripped at the walls and whistled through the cracks. He was glad not be out in the car, wrapped in blankets and huddled on the floor, shaking the dust from his crotch.

"You know what this place was before the war?" Jeremiah asked.

"Not sure. I wasn't here then. But some say a radio station for the Army."

"And what about that other man? Know him?"

"No. Came in off the desert beat to pieces. Real old, too. He hasn't moved much since. By the looks of him, he's from the cities."

His heart did a double-beat, and he took a quick breath.

Having considered giving up on the chase, thinking the old man had died in the wasteland, he was surprised that he'd found the General. The bounty had long expired, but it was the principle that drove him on. He was a man of principles, of his word, about the only thing he had left besides a quick draw and nerves of steel; lose that and he didn't have much, not much at all. "He got any disease?"

Bringing the scarf up over her face, eyes centered on the floor: "We don't care to know people's business around here, sir."

"Well, you should. Know who that is out in the street, or who gunned him down?"

"Him and the other man I got here had a spat and finished it outside." Starting down the hall, turning, Sally asked, "Your name, sir? I like to keep a record."

"Jeremiah'll do."

"Well, Mr. Jeremiah, soup will be up in an hour."

She left, and kicking the piss-pot beneath the bed with a grunt, Jeremiah felt for his rifle and put it within reach. There was a heavy iron skillet in his pack, dented and beat and blasted in, and he tied it around his chest, pulling his dusty shirt down over it.

He'd get some rest and let the dark haze of the desert clear off his brain. There would be plenty time for killing. While they ate was always best.

Jeremiah would have waited to kill the old man in the street, but the wind was fierce and ripped at the walls, rattled the floor. A scarf tied up around his face, desert dust lingered in the air, covered the furniture and the General's shoulders.

It was him. No question.

He was the oldest man Jeremiah had ever seen, much older than he had assumed. His skin looked grey, waxy, like parchment stretched over bone. A small tin bucket, a spit bucket, lay by his feet. It was half-full; he could see tiny flecks of blood on the General's face. He had the cancer, or consumption. And Jeremiah wondered if it would hamper his speed, reaction time, or if he'd even bother to fire back at all. He figured not; he was a notorious assassin and had done in a dozen shootists.

Jeremiah watched his shaking hands lap watery grey soup up into his mouth and glanced at the picture that he kept hidden in his belt: color but badly faded and worn. The old man was younger, in his thirties, with hair, in uniform, smiling, obviously proud.

But it was him. Same fat nose. Same sharp chin. Same long forehead.

Jeremiah pocketed the picture and let instinct take over.

He stepped out from around the corner, firing with his arms extended. The first slug tore into the back wall with a thunk, sending chips of wood flying like shrapnel, plaster dust puffing. Ducking beneath the table, the General threw the soup at the ceiling and went for his piece in one seamless motion. He let off a shot, hitting the doorframe just below Jeremiah's chin and an inch to the left, spitting splinters at his face. Jeremiah emptied the other chamber, splitting the small table down the middle. The old man let out a scream and was sent in a crazy half-roll across the floor, blood spraying.

Jeremiah kicked his gun out of reach, reloaded and put the rifle to the old man's head. He made a wet, blood-choked gurgle, and his eyes went wide as he realized he had drawn his last breath. Jeremiah fired, vaporizing his face in a thunderous blast. Blood and brain and bits of bone sprayed out onto the floor.

He felt no pity as he watched a large dark pool quickly form, things only the dead and terribly maimed could afford or know, and quickly rifled through the General's trousers. There was just a pint of laudanum and three shells for his pistol. In the front pocket of his jacket, he found his identification papers, brown with age. A picture, like the one he carried, was glued to the top right-hand corner, name, rank, serial number listed below.

Screaming, Sally stood in the doorway, clutching her face. "Oh, Lord! What have you done, mister?"

Jeremiah picked up the General's gun, examined it by the lamp. Already cleaned and oiled, he reloaded it, left one chamber empty, spun the cylinder, listened to the soft click as it turned, grinned, and slid it into his belt. "He deserved worse, I assure you. You can have him if you like, or I can drag him out the door for whatever the storm brings through. There's not much left on him, though."

Sally stopped crying, quickly went to the dead man, and pinched his sides for meat. "He'll do," she grinned, already stripping him. "But I'm going to have to ask you to leave, sir."

He scraped up what was left of the soup in the bowl and licked his fingers. "Once the wind lets up, I'll be off again."

She had the old man undressed in a flash and took a dirty carving knife out from her apron, obvious she'd done this many times before. His white legs were surprisingly thick and muscled; she could salt the meat and eat for a month.

"You're not the first to come blasting your way through town." The mechanic handed Jeremiah his boots and picked at a fresh scab on his face. "Guy out in the street didn't take too kindly to Sally being full up, and he didn't take too kindly to being put out, neither. He had it out with that one you just shot up."

The boots were Army-issue, grey, cracked in places, and a size too small, but the best pair he'd had in years. "What about the sandstorms? I hear you've got problems with mutants coming into town scavenging."

"Sure. There's a few. About a week back one went up into the hills after someone plugged it with lead."

"Any rewards?"

The mechanic scratched his chin. "I'm sure we'd be more than grateful if someone was to have a look; might even get offered a place to stay. We've got it bad enough without them making things worse. They get brave when they hang around. I've seen them drag women and children off."

Jeremiah pulled his scarf up, tightened the straps on his pack, and snapped his goggles over his eyes.

Human grease leaking down his face, the mechanic went beneath the hood of the wrecked Buick. It was in pieces now, barely recognizable, guts strewn out across the floor like an explosion had gone off inside it. "Best watch this one. It's good with a gun. Heard it took down two armed men."

He needed rest, and this was the only place to get it. Another few weeks and he'd be ready to push out, but not now. Spitting tar-black chaw, the wind ripping worse than ever, a blizzard of sand and desert grit: "Nothing worse than having to look over your shoulder more than you have to."

"No telling what's gone on with it up there, exposed to the dust like he's been. The stuff's got a way."

Grinning: "Well, I've got a whole belt of bullets says that don't matter none."

Outside, glimpses of the hills could be seen between gusts, a few miles out but not much more, reminding him of ghosts. The mule was buried in dust, a fat pimple on the road. The flies had even left it.

He then saw that the man's body was gone, a quickly fading zigzag trail leading off behind the houses towards the hills.

The storm had calmed. Down past the cracked and twisting one-lane of paved road, he could see the whole of the town, a mere dark-dot of a place, rotted and tilting and surrounded by the endless flat sea of cracked grey.

Squatted down behind a large rock where the twisting road ended and the top of the hill opened up into a flat plateau, Jeremiah could hear it whistling and smell the stench of desert wood burning. If he went in blazing, he would catch it unaware and tear it to pieces.

Gripping both his pistols, he slowly rolled the cylinders to a loaded chamber and cocked both hammers back, his rifle dangling over his chest by a piece of twine.

Flanked on its left side by solid rock, creating a dead end, it was obvious the place had been a small military compound. All that was left were two walls and a cracked and rusted-out radio tower, the rest beaten down and erased by fifty years of desert storms. *NATO, RESTRICTED AREA: AUTHORIZED PERSONNEL ONLY*—worn, faded, and sandblasted—was stenciled in red on the aluminum siding. Another decade and it would all be gone forever, buried in dirt.

He looked out over the rock and had to catch his breath, which felt like a razor, in his throat before he screamed.

Mack.

Was it him? Yes.

But he had changed.

He was naked. Alabaster white, like the belly of a fish, his skin looked wet and bulged with muscle. Twice his normal size, Jeremiah was sure Mack could crush him with his bare hands, break and snap his every bone.

Mack was roasting the body he had dragged off from town. It was black and burned, and the fire spat as grease dripped.

Gripping the pistols, sweat pouring, Jeremiah leapt out, guns blazing and going off like dynamite inside his head, sparks and smoke spitting out the end of the barrel. Jeremiah's first bullet tore into Mack's side and exited his back. The next three missed by inches, opening small dime-sized holes in the aluminum wall. Clutching at the pit of his stomach, blood pumping out between his fingers, two more bullets found a home. Jeremiah let off another two rounds; one went wild, the other pierced the centre of Mack's chest. He fell over sideways, and Jeremiah knew it'd cracked his sternum, maybe ricocheted and busted his heart or his right lung wide open.

Mack let out two last quick gasps, slumped to the side, and went silent, his eyes wide and staring.

Cordite was thick in the air, and Jeremiah's shoulders ached from the kick of the pistols. He holstered them.

He wouldn't make the same mistake twice. Clutching his .30-30, he stepped forward, the barrel aimed squarely at Mack's head.

There was a click, metal on metal, then a sharp, blinding pain bit into his right leg, crippling him. He looked down and saw a tripwire running across the width of the path. A meat cleaver, tied to the end of a stick, had snapped around and was now buried in his right shin, digging an inch deep into his tibia.

He pried it free, wanting to scream, but bit down on his lip until he tasted blood.

Laughing, Mack said, "Dinner's served."

Jeremiah looked up.

The red dots had vanished, had healed themselves miraculously, and Jeremiah knew he was about to die. On Mack's left side, where he'd been blasted open months ago, was a greasy third arm, not much more than a stump with fingers, which brandished a cannon of a revolver.

Jeremiah stared at the dark eye of the barrel, saw the cylinder turn over, sparks flash, heard the sharp clap, and he was finished.

Author's Notes

Exposed!

Essentially, this short story was an exercise in restraint. There are several scenes where the characters are involved in the television show, either as participants or viewers. I could have written more—far more. There was some juicy, juicy stuff rattling around in my brain, but I felt that another scene or two, although fun to write, would have hurt the flow of the narrative. Less *was* more.

The inspiration came from Atwood's *The Handmaid's Tale* and Orwell's *1984*. And, like them, the central character—*was Jerry; now Jake*—is nobody, an everyman, who suffers through what most surely suffer through: poverty, alienation, fear. His goal is survival, not advancement, and he dreams of a time when love and friendship were valued. I wanted his eyes to show you the grime behind the glamour of utopia, the stink, the rot, the corrupting nature of money and material possessions, of conformity. He hasn't been hypnotized by their devices. It's a theme running through a lot of my work.

Hard as Rock

St. John's is a small city. Last count, there was something like only a hundred thousand of us. Because of this, we don't have many of the same serious economic and social problems that plague other larger Atlantic Canadian cities, like Halifax. It's only been recently that homelessness has even been brought to the forefront of the news media, and this is due to rising drug problems and violence associated with them, not for the health and living standards of the homeless. But the point is that the main character is an anomaly and a visible target.

We've had several "hobos" that everyone knows or at least knows *of*, who have become part of our urban folk landscape: Hole in the Cake, Raymond the Hatter, Silly Willie, Stewart Taylor, and Tommy Toe. It's rumored, and there's nothing to verify this other than the collective memory of the community, that he was buried alive in the foundation of the main overpass when it was built in the 1960s. There was a rapid industrialization of the city's infrastructure during that period, and safety standards were surely overlooked for the good of progress, making his tragic story somewhat plausible.

Whether or not there's any truth to this is irrelevant; the image of a man walking the city streets still half incased in concrete—an idea I've had rumbling around in one capacity or another for years—was something I couldn't pass up any longer.

I saw him as a Frankenstein figure, an anti-hero, lonely and desperate. And although his actions are violent and grotesque, I wanted the reader to identify with him nonetheless. Like many of my stories, this is a tale of "just deserts," a *Tales from the Crypt* episode on some bad acid.

Home Is Where the Heart Is

I remember flicking through the stations, stopping at CNN and watching people cling to roofs, helicopters dotting the sky, countless down-turned bodies and garbage floating through neighborhoods that had merged into a swelling sea. I thought, *This must be India. Malaysia, maybe. It certainly isn't here. Things like this don't happen in the West.* Then the ticker told me that it was New Orleans. More footage shot at me: people pouring out of shopping centres, arms full of stolen goods, police standing around, eyes blaring, looking confused and frightened. Total and complete anarchy.

Notch another monumental human disaster that could have been avoided.

I felt a deep sadness for those people, which only grew as conditions worsened and the death toll mounted.

Amongst all the confusion, there was a story to be told. And hearing men and women cry and weep about how their fathers and mothers and daughters and sons drowned in their living rooms ripped me apart inside.

I had to write on this.

Horror is always at the forefront of modern literature. We take risks. Nothing is taboo. By no means am I treading new ground, and I don't claim to be, but I thought that a great starting point for a short story was the notion that this human catastrophe was so great that something, something beyond our understanding, had to have sway over it.

The plot came to me almost immediately: something was lurking in that greasy, black water, feeding on the desperate.

Whenever I think of the sea, I think Lovecraft. Like vampires and zombies, tentacles and unknowable beasts from the deep are staples of the genre, and we continue to revisit and reinvent them. They never get tired.

Cold Deck

A significant number of small communities within Newfoundland and Labrador are supported by a single company, and they have become a life-blood.

There is an estimated seven thousand people in the Stephenville area, of which over three hundred were employed in the local newsprint mill. In December 2005, it closed its doors permanently, leaving many to either move to the mainland in search of employment or depend on the limited government assistance available to them.

I knew there was a story here. But pitchfork, torch-wielding mobs of the proletariat seemed far too obvious. I had an idea of a man with chainsaw hands, but there was no story, just the image. I've heard countless fish-plant workers complain that they've given up their health to feed their families, having surgery after surgery to repair cartilage damage and back problems caused by decades packaging crab legs or cod fillets on a conveyer belt. Logging's still a thriving industry here, I told myself, so why not have the protagonists as loggers, have them give up their limbs to be replaced by tools.

The rest came easy. I just had to keep it grounded in some semblance of Newfoundland culture. I did not want fantasy in any way.

The only snag was the dialogue. Some writers are masters of it. I'm not. The problem was that I had to bridge the gap between the rich dialects of Newfoundland and the story I had to tell. Like most of my writing, I tried to create a staccato beat, as if you're reading a police report or something off the wire, while at the same time I tired to infuse it with some of the idioms unique to the province and the logging industry. I hope it worked.

Stains of Life

It's funny how a story can take you places, transform itself into something wholly and completely different than originally envisioned. Stephen King has called this "digging."

Public transportation. That's where this one started—on the bus. Standing at the terminal, in the gloom of fall, people wait, smoke, hop from foot to foot. Some are patients at the local mental health facility down the road, quite a few, in fact. They constantly mull around the local shopping centre, begging for change, picking soggy butts off the ground, inspecting them. I've always viewed them with a certain amount of pity and fascination.

At the outset, I thought that maybe the bus could take me, as well as the other passengers, to some windswept and barren dimension, something out of Lovecraft or from Fulci's *The Beyond*. But what struck me most was the number of people smoking, hacking up their lungs, spitting. I'd been reading Huxley's *Brave New World* at the time, and it seemed obvious to me, as I sat through the considerable ride, that if this was a world like that, they'd be dead by now, euthanized. Where governments have no restraint, why would they spend billions on cancer treatment, addiction counseling, when they could simply murder the "undesirables"? For me, as a student of German history, the gas vans of Chelmno and the Fordist, factory style death of Auschwitz aren't that far removed from *our* society.

Beneath Ground

Cannibals and zombies have much in common, other than the obvious. They offer important social commentaries. *Dawn of the Dead* spoke of how we're on the path to becoming a nation of slaves. *Raw Meat*, however, which inspired this story, is about social revolution. The same could be said for Jack Ketchum's *Off Season* and *Offspring*, as well as *The Hills Have Eyes*. Their villains, abandoned by society, prey upon the rich, educated, middle class, and their victims are editors, bankers, students, policemen. They eat flesh, not to consume them for nourishment, but as a subconscious act of rebellion, a proverbial middle finger stuck up to the world.

Miners, lepers, prostitutes, abused and neglected children, they once occupied the lowest positions in our society, making this point abundantly clear.

I did reveal the origins of the cannibals in an earlier version of "Beneath Ground." They were young and poor and desperate and dug into the earth to *get away from it all*. I came to realize—and was advised through a friendly and helpful rejection letter—that this section hurt the tone and pace of the story, since I wanted it to read like an anxiety attack. Removing it hurt nothing. The sub-text is obvious, since the victims here are the upwardly mobile and a landlord.

Open 24/7

You write what you know. Insomnia is something I know well; it's a close personal friend of mine. We've been through a lot, insomnia and I, more than I care to divulge. But some of it's here, in this story, just twisted a little.

For six months, I worked overnights at a corner-store, banging out stories sitting on a plastic milk-crate, notebook resting on my knees. Reality becomes some vague and hazy dream when you don't sleep. You forget things, become irrational, paranoid, lose weight. Daily routine is a never-ending struggle. You feel isolated from your friends and family.

Like Stephen King's *Insomnia*, lack of sleep opens the third eye, if you want to call it that. Lovecraft heavily influenced this piece, too, where dreams are doorways and the supernatural lies in wait just beyond our reality and shadowy figures are harbingers of doom. Here they're crusty alcoholics.

Starved to Death

Popular culture likes to victimize women, make them into targets and bombard them with images of unattainable physical perfection. It's constant, unabated, infiltrating every form of entertainment and advertisement, and reinforced by our icons. Size 2 is the new fat; Botox is the new Mary Kay.

Men are no exception. Performance enhancing drugs are commonplace among college students and silicone implants are becoming increasingly popular with yuppies.

In that sense, both of the characters in this story are victims, and many of the traits exhibited by Byron started out as Pricilla's. But for me, that was too predictable and played on too many stereotypes. And it was easy. Switching it around gave the story something fresh, I hope, and took it in a new direction. Originally, Byron took the drugs, and after some bizarre reaction, ate Pricilla. *The Age of Desire*, maybe, with the addition of a human Big Mac.

Dancers in the Dark

Since reading John Coyne's *The Hunting Season*, I wanted to write a short story set in rural Appalachia, but stripped down to the basics, to the things we can all relate to: isolation, poverty, family. I knew the landscape and their eccentric cultural rituals could be manipulated easily enough to create tone and atmosphere, but I didn't want an outsider looking in, a common trope in popular horror. A member of my imagined small community, reexamining their place in it, seemed far more interesting.

The question of who this person was and why he was telling his story, *their* story, plagued me for months. It wasn't until my father gave me a copy of Shelby Lee Adams' *Appalachian Legacy*—haunting black-and-white portraits filled with seas of shadows, portraits that are themselves microcosms of daily life in rural Kentucky—that the pieces fell into place and I found my characters.

They're all there: Brice, Doc Sam, Maggie. Even the shotgun blast to the stomach is recounted in some detail by Adams.

He makes it clear that the mystery of religion is a large part of their lives, particularly Pentecostal snake handling, and seemed to have stemmed from the move to industrial capitalism or coal mining. I tried to integrate that same mystery into this piece, which is why the mine figures largely and could be seen as a metaphor for the intrusion of *our* society on *theirs*.

The Last Highwayman

The concept of a highwayman, at least as far as I can determine, came from Pat Frank's *Alas, Babylon*. For me, it brought to mind images of stagecoaches and drunken, rotten-toothed marauders and John Ford films. And in certain respects, this tale *is* a Western. It has many of the staples of that genre: barren desert, dusty town, stern landlady, shootouts. And like many of the protagonists of the Spaghetti Western, Jeremiah is a solitary figure, often violent, and prone to using his pistols. The language pays homage to the work of L'Amour and Swarthout, or maybe it's just some vague attempt at flattery on my part.

That is where the similarities end.

Jeremiah's world is a nuclear wasteland full of radioactive desert-dust, cancer, mutants and cannibalism, and has more to do with the sci-fi apocalyptic scare-fare of the 1950s than horse spurs and saloons. Essentially, Jeremiah is a vehicle to display the darkest parts of a future society, but it's more style than substance.

Bombed-out cities, dead animals, and cannibalism are touched on in varying degrees of detail to develop the tone and atmosphere, which I hoped would weigh on the reader like a disease. But I leave much to the imagination; exposition is the bane of the horror writer.

About the Author

Born and raised in the historic harbor city of St. John's, Newfoundland, the oldest city in North America, Mike Heffernan has been poking his nose around in the darker side of the human condition for as long as he can remember. He thinks he can pinpoint his baptism in blood to primary school, when his cousin subjected him to an almost daily dose of a deadly cocktail of horror movies.

Mike later cut his teeth on such nastiness as Barker, Skipp and Spector, Romero and King. Writing since his adolescence, he put his creative endeavors on hold to study German history, but came back to horror with a mean vengeance. It's been full-tilt-boogie for some time now, and it seems to be panning out. His books include *Aim for the Head*, *A Dark and Deadly Valley*, and *Exposed*.

About Silverthought Press

Silverthought Press is an independent publishing company based in Northern New York. Paul Hughes (*Enemy*, *An End*, *Broken: A Plague Journal*) launched silverthought.com in 2001 as a venue where writers of speculative fiction gather, display, and discuss their work. Since its print division's debut in 2005, Silverthought's releases have been the recipients of honors from some of the most esteemed competitions in the field of independent publishing, including the Independent Publisher Book Award and the DIY Book Festival Award.

For more information, please visit www.silverthought.com.